"DOESN'T YOUR CONSCIENCE BOTHER YOU AT ALL?" JOHN MICHAEL ASKED, A CYNICAL SMILE ON HIS FACE.

"Should it?" Barbara demanded, startled by his question.

"I think mine would," he said slowly, holding her eyes with his. "I believe I would feel quite bad about taking advantage of two elderly ladies the way you're taking advantage of my aunts. You know the book they're paying you to write for them will never be published."

"We'll see about that, Mr. Stewart," she said haughtily. Barbara glared at him for an instant then dropped her gaze. The tension between them was becoming unbearable.

"I merely want you to be reasonable, Miss Whitney," he said, reaching out for her arm. His voice was low and sounded almost dangerous. "But I want you to be aware that if you insist on writing this book, I'm going to fight you every inch of the way."

CANDLELIGHT ECSTASY ROMANCES®

SOUTHERN FIRE

Jo Calloway

A CANDLELIGHT ECSTASY ROMANCE®

Published by
Dell Publishing Co., Inc.
1 Dag Hammarskjold Plaza
New York, New York 10017

ISBN: 0-440-18170-4

Printed in the United States of America

First printing—October 1985

To Our Readers:

We have been delighted with your enthusiastic response to Candlelight Ecstasy Romances®, and we thank you for the interest you have shown in this exciting series.

In the upcoming months we will continue to present the distinctive sensuous love stories you have come to expect only from Ecstasy. We look forward to bringing you many more books from your favorite authors and also the very finest work from new authors of contemporary romantic fiction.

As always, we are striving to present the unique, absorbing love stories that you enjoy most—books that are more than ordinary romance. Your suggestions and comments are always welcome. Please write to us at the address below.

Sincerely,

The Editors
Candlelight Romances
1 Dag Hammarskjold Plaza
New York, New York 10017

CHAPTER ONE

Barbara Whitney groaned heavily, flexing her weary fingers as she shifted positions in the leather seat. Morosely she looked to the right, then to the left before turning north on the two-lane highway. Her body ached dully from the three-day trip into the Deep South. Glancing at the folded map on the console, she tried to calculate how much farther she had to travel before reaching her destination.

Suddenly she laughed, pushing her fingers through her curly brown hair and gripping the side of her head. But her laughter quickly died, and her light blue eyes ceased dancing as she muttered, "I must have lost my mind." She looked out to the side of the highway at the freshly plowed fields of rich brown soil. If even a month ago anyone had told her that June 1 would find her stopping to ask directions to the Stewart house in Baldwyn, Mississippi, she would have regarded such an announcement with sheer amusement. Yet here she was, pulling her packed twenty-year-old Volkswagen into the first gas station she saw as she entered the small southern town.

Of course, for the past thousand miles, all the way from her home in Trenton, New Jersey, she had continuously promised and sworn to herself that this would be her first and last such trip. There was only so much she would do for money, and she had already decided she had just about hit the limit.

She steered the car in front of the gas pumps and halted, glancing in the direction of the building.

A dark-haired, dour-faced young man, wearing oil-stained denims and a shirt that Barbara assumed was supposed to be white, walked lazily from the door of the station. "Fill 'er up?" he called out, approaching Barbara's side of the car.

"Oh, no," she said, tilting her head to one side at the young man and smiling pleasantly. "I'd like a little information."

"Well, this is a gas station, lady. If you're not buying gas, then you need to pull on away from the pumps so our cash-paying customers can get in."

"Oh, excuse me," Barbara stammered, her large blue eyes rounding. Quickly she shifted into drive and moved the car. Halting at the far side of the concrete lot, she opened her door, got out, and walked back toward the pumps, where the abrasive young man stood.

He laughed. "Sure don't see many of those old Volkswagens anymore. How old is it?"

"Twenty years," Barbara replied tolerantly, squinting in response to the bright sun.

"And that thing made it all the way from New Jersey?" he said chidingly, his eyes twinkling now.

Her face felt very warm. "Yes," she answered a little curtly, in defense of her tried and true VW. From the appearance of his beat-up old pickup squatting beside the building, she didn't believe he had a valid reason to be laughing at her car. Almost biting her tongue, she asked politely, "Could you tell me where Brice Road is located?"

He pointed north. "Left turn at the first red light."

"Could you tell me where I might find the Stewart house?"

He sniffed and touched one side of his nose. "Nope. Never heard of it."

Startled, Barbara exclaimed, "Why, that's impossible! They've been here for more than a hundred years."

He shrugged, unimpressed by her announcement. "Could be. But I've been here only two weeks. I'm from up the road a ways. I'm down here working for my uncle during the summer.

11

To be honest, I don't know that much about this town."

Barbara felt her insides churning with frustration. Why had he wasted her time? Having driven across this sultry country with no air conditioning in her car, she felt like a wilted lily. The three-day road trip had worn her down. Now irritated and agitated, she was half tempted to turn around and head back home. Her desire for a time of self-exploration might be waning from its peak; in fact, it might be dying completely. She regretted ever having picked up that magazine and having read the classified section. "Well, thank you," she said, then turned back toward her car.

"If you want, I could go inside and ask my uncle about the place. He'd know," the gas attendant called out to her.

Barbara stopped cold and looked around. Then her gaze went to the large dirty window of the station. Sure enough, behind the desk, with his feet propped on it, sat another man. "If it wouldn't be too much trouble, I would appreciate it." She then stood waiting in the hot sun while the young man ambled into the station. She watched him say something to the older man. A moment passed, and the feet slid from the desk. Then the young man came out the door, followed by his uncle.

"You want to know about the Stewart house?" the older man asked gruffly.

"Yes," Barbara replied politely. "I would like to know how to get there."

"You kin to the ladies?" His bushy brows raised in question.

She felt herself growing a bit leery, and she was beginning to resent the fact that she couldn't seem to get a simple question answered. "No," she answered without elaborating.

"Well, you know they're real old. For a fact nobody around here knows how old they are. But we all know neither one of them is too bright in the head."

I should fit right in, Barbara thought. *I'm only twenty-nine, but obviously I'm not too bright in the head either, or I wouldn't be standing here.* With exaggerated politeness she asked, "Could you tell me how to get there please?"

Scratching his head, the older man said, "Take a left at the red light. It's the first house on the right. But look close 'cause it's way off the road and hid behind a bunch of shrubs and trees."

Barbara breathed a sigh of relief. "Thank you," she said. Then she turned toward her car.

The owner called out, "If you're here trying to buy their antiques, you'll be wasting your time. Those two old maids have had people from all over the world trying to buy from them, but they're so tight they wouldn't let go of nothing for any price. Of course, they don't need the

13

money." Suddenly he stopped, as if he'd already said more than he intended. Both men stood staring while Barbara started the noisy motor, then slowly pulled the burdened little car back onto the highway. She ran her fingers through her curly hair, feeling the perspiration at the sides of her face. *I may have done it this time. I really may have.*

From her rearview mirror she could see both men watching as she made her left turn at the red light. But once away from their glares, she slowed down, stopped the car, and gave her face a quick once-over in the small mirror, peering critically at the fair skin, at the delicate facial bones accentuated by dark brows and black lashes, close-cropped hair, and dry full lips. She took a lipstick from her purse and gave herself a new coat of bright red before realizing she'd pulled out the wrong tube. She quickly wiped at her lips with a tissue, then took the tissue and rubbed a little blush onto her cheeks. This trip had about killed her.

She missed the drive, crowded with vines and bushes, and had to back up. She turned slowly off the street, not at all sure of the emotion she felt. From the appearance of the drive she had just discovered an ideal location to film *Psycho III*. Slowing even more, she shifted her slender body uncomfortably in her seat, edging at a snail's pace along the brick drive.

Then, suddenly emerging into a clearing, she

stopped the car dead still. There before her eyes was the largest old antebellum house she'd ever seen: three stories high with columns so large she couldn't reach around one with both arms. Amazingly enough, it appeared to be in very good condition. Freshly painted, it was an enormous southern palace hidden neatly behind a veil of greenery. A most extraordinary sight indeed.

Inhaling a deep breath, Barbara took her foot off the brake and slowly approached the front steps of a tremendous porch, which was ten times longer than her car, or maybe twenty times. She'd never seen such a house except maybe in pictures of those occupied by America's wealthiest families.

The moment she switched off the motor, the huge door of the house swung open, and two elderly ladies appeared side by side, staring down onto the drive. Self-consciously Barbara opened the door and got out. She brushed the wrinkles from her clothes before stepping around the car to greet the two women. "Hello," she said, smiling warmly. "I'm Barbara Whitney." She half waved, then slid both hands into the pockets of her skirt. Trying not to stare, she took quick note that the women resembled each other greatly; both had their hair parted in the middle with waves along the sides and drawn back and securely knotted at their napes. Straight out of the twenties.

15

"Hello, dear." One spoke. "We've been expecting you for days now." She gestured with one hand for Barbara to come up onto the porch.

Barbara's stiff legs carried her cautiously up the large brick steps and onto the enormous tile porch. Touching somewhat nervously at the base of her neck, she said, "It's terribly warm in the South, isn't it?"

"Oh, yes," the taller woman responded happily. "But it's good for you. So many of the body's poisons are washed away by perspiration. Our own sweet father lived to be ninety-six before he passed on. And he was such a perspirer. For a fact he—"

"Shhh, Henrietta," the other interrupted. "Let poor dead Papa rest."

Barbara moved in fairly close for the introductions. "I'm Henrietta Stewart, and this is my sister, Hannah."

Barbara extended her hand first to one woman, then to the other, saying, "Nice to meet you." In her mind she was saying, *Henrietta is the taller one with less gray in her hair.* "Miss Henrietta and Miss Hannah."

"And it's nice to meet you, dear," Hannah said, smiling with delight. "It seems we have been waiting a long time for this moment."

"Yes, we have," Henrietta added. "Now, come inside and we'll have a glass of tea." Turning to her sister, she said, "You'd better call John Mi-

16

chael. He said he wanted to know the moment Miss Whitney arrived. Let's don't get him riled here at the start."

A questioning expression on her face, Barbara followed the two women inside. Then she halted on the beige marble-floored entrance hall, her lips parting in surprise. To the right was a beautiful staircase with an elaborately carved balustrade, and along the stairs on the walls were magnificent landscapes and still lifes from time long passed. Directly across was the reception room, or living room, with Louis XIV furnishings on a deep crimson rug. In a glance Barbara saw ivory, marble, silver, a roomful of priceless antiques.

"Come on, dear," Henrietta said, taking a gentle hold on Barbara's arm. "We'll go into the dining room, and Hannah will join us after she calls John Michael."

Barbara nodded and accompanied the spry woman down the wide hallway. They walked to large French doors opening into a dining room which could have easily seated fifty guests. She quickly eyed the priceless chandelier hanging above the table, thinking, *What a lovely old home.*

"Lila," Henrietta called out toward the single door at the north end of the room, "we're here."

A slightly overweight middle-aged woman came through the door into the dining room.

She smiled pleasantly at Barbara, then at Henrietta. "Tea?" she asked, knowing the answer.

"Yes. Also bring a glass for Hannah. She's calling John Michael."

Lila nodded and disappeared back into the kitchen, humming under her breath.

"Sit, sit." Henrietta motioned to Barbara.

Barbara pulled out a gold upholstered chair and seated herself. Inhaling a deep breath, she looked down the full length of the long polished table, then back to Henrietta Stewart, who had taken a chair directly across from her. Obviously these two women had more wealth than anyone Barbara had met in her life, so the proposed project ahead didn't make a lot of sense to her.

The tea was served, and Henrietta said, "Thank you, Lila. You might want to begin preparing lunch."

Rolling her eyes, the woman, Lila, said, "Miss Henrietta, I started lunch at seven this morning. Don't you remember? You came down and told me to put on a roast."

"Oh, so I did." Henrietta laughed, looking up at Lila. "Don't pay any mind to me, Lila. I'm just so excited over Miss Whitney's arrival."

At that moment Hannah entered the dining room and went to the chair beside her sister. Leaning over a bit toward her, she whispered loudly, "He's uspet."

"Oh, dear," Henrietta said. "I thought he would be reconciled to it by now."

The whispers were so loud that Barbara had no difficulty overhearing the brisk conversation taking place across the table. But she sipped her tea, fighting back the question "Who is John Michael?"

Finally the whispers ended, and Hannah looked up at Barbara. "Are you a northerner by birth, dear?" she asked bluntly.

Barbara straightened. "Yes. Born and bred in New Jersey."

"North or South New Jersey?" Henrietta asked, smiling with perfectly sculptured white dentures.

Barbara was thoughtful for a moment. "Uh, Trenton. It's—"

Before she could continue, Hannah interrupted. "That's good enough for me. I've always wanted to visit New Jersey, and I'm sure having you here will be like a visit."

Henrietta smiled in agreement.

Hannah leaned forward. "When can we begin? I'm so anxious I can hardly contain myself."

Henrietta kind of shivered and covered a gleeful laugh with one hand.

Barbara lowered her glass to the table. "I suppose I should first find a motel and check in. Perhaps in the morning we could begin with an outline."

"You'll do no such thing. You'll stay right here with us," Henrietta Stewart announced with emphasis. "We already have your room prepared." She inhaled deeply. "It'll be delightful to have a lovely young woman in the house. It's been such a long time since we had a guest, and we've never had one from New Jersey."

"But I had planned—"

"We won't hear of it," Hannah said, raising both hands. Her voice was level, sincere. "Besides, dear, we don't have a decent motel anymore. What we do have is a not very respectable truck stop north of town where truck drivers take their women. It's just a blight on the town, but we'll tell you more about it later."

Henrietta concurred readily, adding grimly, "It's a bad place. I don't believe you'd be happy there."

Barbara followed their conversation with her eyes. With a self-conscious smile she said, "In that event I'll accept your generous offer to stay here."

"Good for you," Henrietta said, then sipped gracefully from her glass. "Lila!" she yelled unexpectedly.

The door swung open again, and the woman appeared, a blank expression on her face.

"Lila, would you help Miss Whitney unload her car and take her things up to the guest room on the third floor?"

Hannah looked to Barbara. "We've given you the entire floor so you can set up your office and have all the room you need."

Lila put one hand on her hip, sighing with

obvious disgust. "Do you want me to cook dinner or do you want me to stop dinner and go unload the car?" She glared firmly at one Stewart woman, then at the other.

Barbara interjected, "Oh, listen, I don't need any help. I can unload the car. Please go on with what you're doing."

With a grunt the woman backed into the kitchen and disappeared.

"I don't know what we'd do without Lila." Henrietta smiled at Barbara. "Good help is so hard to find these days. Of course, John Michael found her for us. And she's been here for three years. Came on her fiftieth birthday, and we had a party to celebrate." She leaned forward and whispered, "Her husband, Rufus, is in the pen at Parchman. Got caught passing bad checks for the fourth time. John Michael's trying to get him paroled, but he hasn't had much luck so far. The parole board can be obstinate when it wants to be. However, we've promised Lila to hire him to keep the yard and garden. Maybe we can keep him clean that way."

Barbara covered her mouth with her fingers, fighting back the smile, the laughter bubbling up inside her. What in the world had she done!

The squeal of tires at the front of the house caused all three women to straighten in their chairs. "That's John Michael." Henrietta slid her eyes to her sister.

21

" 'Fraid so." Hannah agreed with a nod of her head. "Sure didn't take him long to get here."

Finally Barbara couldn't stand it a moment longer. She leaned forward, whispering, "Who's John Michael?" just as the entrance door slammed and quick, heavy steps sounded along the hall.

"Dear, we're in the dining room," Henrietta called sweetly.

The French doors swung open, and Barbara jerked around to stare straight into the face of a tall, deeply bronzed golden-haired man, his slate blue eyes glaring directly at her. "Are you the ghostwriter?" he asked brusquely. He looked severe and broodingly unhappy to see her.

Appalled, she answered a soft "Yes."

He inclined his head slightly in the direction of the two women seated across from her. "Aunt Henri, Aunt Hannah, please excuse us a moment, will you?" Then he motioned to Barbara, saying, "Would you please step out here with me?"

She rose from the chair, thinking, *So this is John Michael.* He had called the women Aunt, she noted. With an anxious look on her face she glanced quickly at the two elderly matrons, who were eyeing each other and shrugging. Feeling keenly abandoned, Barbara walked from the room, closing the door behind her.

John Michael moved several steps down the

hall, a safe earshot from the dining room, and stood near the staircase. "Miss?" His neat brows raised.

"Whitney," she answered.

"Miss Whitney," he said simply, "do you know why you're here?" Dressed in a three-piece suit, John Michael was a very attractive man, sturdily and rather generously built with impressive shoulders and a nicely tapered body.

There was a pause before Barbara remarked, "Yes. I'm here to help those women in there"— she gestured toward the dining room with her head, then added—"write a book." She was staring into the most beautiful irises she had ever seen, the color of the sea on a pretty, sunshiny day, and an expression which carried the majesty and power of the sea.

Before she could proceed, his sensual lips curled in a near smile. "Not any book," he said. "They have a special book in mind."

"Oh?" She stared blankly at him. "I didn't know. We haven't had time to discuss the material."

"I don't want you to help with the writing of this book," he said in a soft but stern tone.

She drew back, surprised. "What?"

"No, I don't, because if you do, they'll most likely spend the remainder of their lives in court."

She struggled to comprehend his words and,

23

after a moment, said, "I'm afraid I don't understand."

"Well"—he touched the corner of one eye—"let me see if I can explain it to you." He paused. "Last summer Aunt Henrietta bought a copy of *Peyton Place* at the secondhand bookstore in Corinth. She read it, and then she passed it on to Aunt Hannah."

Barbara stood in sober silence, listening.

"At some point during the winter they decided that Baldwyn, Mississippi, could easily be transformed into a southern Peyton Place. They decided to, as they put it, 'spill the beans' about this community. That's when they advertised in that writers' magazine for a ghostwriter."

"I see," Barbara said very softly, watching him closely.

He continued. "I am prepared to pay you for your time and expenses if you will kindly inform them you've changed your mind."

After a long pause she shook her curly head energetically. "But I haven't. I was hired to assist your aunts in writing a book, and that's exactly what I intend to do—write a book," she said stubbornly.

He flushed, then gave her a hard stare.

She did not flinch under his gaze.

"All right, Miss Whitney," he said dryly. "Do what you think is best, but be prepared to spend the remainder of your life in the South defending yourself. I didn't become an attorney to

24

spend my time in court fighting libel suits, especially suits brought on by members of my own hardheaded family." After turning abruptly, he stepped down the hallway in long strides, then stopped at the door and glanced back. "Remember, I warned you."

She smiled easily. "I'll remember."

He slammed the door behind him.

She stood for a moment looking at the beautiful stained glass of the front doors, then turned slowly back toward the dining room, where the co-conspirators waited.

CHAPTER TWO

Barbara fell backward and stretched out on the gigantic four-poster bed in the middle of the oversize room, gazing up at the high, high ceiling. Somewhere deep inside her a laugh was developing, a joyful bubble springing outward. The pillow under her head was huge, soft, stuffed with feathers, as was the mattress, which became sculptured to her trim body. Lying on the bed, head deep in the pillow, was much like floating on air, a strangely comforting feeling.

She turned her head slightly to the right and looked at the suitcases on the floor. After the meeting with the beloved nephew she didn't know if it was wise to go ahead and begin unpacking. She closed her eyes and lay quietly. She didn't know what to think or do, so she laughed inwardly and shook her head. Perhaps it was the tiresome journey, but she felt a little giddy and strangely off-balance.

Suddenly she sat up, swung her feet off the sides of the bed, and laughed aloud. She had the entire third floor of this lovely old house at her disposal: bedroom, sitting room, large bath on one side of the hallway, and, on the opposite side, two adjoining rooms set up for her work area, complete with manual typewriter, file cabinets, antique desk, sofa. It was much more than she had imagined in her wildest thoughts.

Moving from the bed, she walked to the doors which led onto the balcony and, pulling them open, looked out across the Stewart land, at the trees in the distance, many tangled with vines and ivy. She filled her lungs with the warm air, then closed the doors and looked back at the bags on the floor. A moment later she began to unpack, taking the clothes from the bag to the dresser, to the huge walk-in closet strong with the scent of cedar. It was difficult to believe that only one short week ago she had been visiting her sister in the hospital, looking through the nursery glass at her newest niece. A middle child in a large family, Barbara had become accustomed to visits to the hospital to view her newest relatives. Little Ginger's arrival last week brought the tally to fifteen nieces and nephews, so she needed this job if for no other reason than to buy Christmas presents.

During past summers Barbara had usually taken postgraduate courses and spent the remaining few weeks in a New Jersey beach house, sharing expenses with two friends. It was moments precisely like this one that made her wonder if she'd bitten off more than she could even put in her mouth, least of all chew. The one thing she knew for certain about novels was that she'd never written one. And here she was a thousand miles from home, pen in hand, getting ready to tackle a really big job. A little smile played at her mouth as she thought of the overprotective nephew with his worried scowl. If he really knew how slim the chances of this endeavor's amounting to anything were, he would relax and maybe even smile. Of course, the elderly author of . . . *And the Ladies of the Club* had hit the jackpot, but she was to publishing what Grandma Moses was to painting—a unique occurrence.

After refreshing herself with a bath, Barbara put on baggy jeans and a sweater. She was drying her hair when a knock sounded on the door. "Come in," she called cheerily, placing the dryer on the dresser and picking up her brush.

"Dear?" Henrietta Stewart peered inside.

"Come on in." Barbara smiled warmly, a question in her mind about the identity of her caller. With the two women apart it was difficult to discern who was who.

"Do you think you'll be comfortable?" Henrietta asked, closing the door behind her.

"Oh, yes. It's beautiful." Barbara laughed, pushing the brush through her hair, then plac-

29

ing it back on the dresser. "This is such a lovely place, but I could have made do with much less room."

"Hannah and I wanted the very best for you, dear," Henrietta announced with a twinkle in her eyes. She hesitated, then said cautiously, "Tell me, do you think we might begin after dinner this evening?"

"Yes." Barbara agreed readily. "I see no reason why not. I'm anxious to begin."

Clasping her hands together above her breasts, Henrietta chuckled. "Oh, so are we. It's so exciting. But we didn't want to overtire you. We know how far you've come."

"I feel fine," Barbara said. "The bath did wonders, and this room is so refreshing. I love this furniture."

Henrietta's proud gaze went around the room, then paused as she said pleasantly, "I see you've tried out the bed." Barbara's imprint on the feather mattress remained clearly visible.

Barbara flushed, admitting, "I couldn't help myself. I've never seen a bed so tall or so lush. It was like stretching out on a cloud."

Henrietta smiled slightly. "John Michael's, uh, wife used to say sleeping in this bed made her feel like Scarlett O'Hara."

Barbara's eyes widened. Oh, well, just how stupid could she be? Of course, the man had to be married. Still, the information upset her momentarily. Finally she said, "I can understand how she would feel that way. The nostalgia is almost tangible."

Henrietta nodded and started back toward the door. "Dinner is at six," she stated matter-of-factly, then added, "That is, if Lila's running on schedule. Sometimes we have to make allowances for the poor thing. She's right in the middle of menopause." Henrietta sighed aloud. "And to be truthful, Hannah and I both believe it's the worst case we've ever seen."

The door closed, and Barbara stood staring with a look of amused bewilderment on her face. Then she turned and went over to the bed and straightened the spread, toying with the thought that John Michael and his wife had slept here. Without understanding the motive, for some unknown reason, the knowledge filled her with an odd sensation.

A few minutes before six she left the third floor and started down the stairs. She stopped on the second-floor landing and glanced down the hallway to see Hannah Stewart coming out of a room. When she noticed Barbara, Hannah gave a little wave with a white linen handkerchief and said pleasantly, "Good evening, dear."

Barbara waited for her on the landing, and after a moment the two started down the stairs together. About midway Hannah said, "I was just preparing a room for John Michael. He called a little while ago to say he needed to stay in town for a couple of days, some big court case,

I suppose. He is the best lawyer between here and Memphis."

Barbara glanced quizzically but made no comment, though she couldn't help wondering if his wife would join him in the overnight stay. Walking side by side with Hannah toward the dining room, Barbara smelled a remarkably pleasing aroma.

"That doesn't smell much like roast, does it, dear?" Hannah glanced upward at Barbara.

Barbara smiled at the comment. "No, I would say it smells more like lasagna or spaghetti." If it *was* a roast, Lila had certainly sprinkled some heavy seasoning on it.

"Oh, goodness," Hannah muttered, entering the dining room. Immediately Henrietta bent forward across the table and whispered, "Lila scorched the roast."

And when Hannah started to respond, Henrietta put two fingers to her mouth, saying, "Shhh. Now don't upset her, Hannah. Poor thing is upset enough already."

"But, Henrietta," Hannah said in a low voice, "she's burned up everything for a week, and I'm getting tired of ravioli." She seated herself and motioned for Barbara to be seated too. Then, with a prim expression on her face, she rolled her eyes to the ceiling and announced, "Lila, we're ready."

All eyes turned to the door in less than anxious anticipation. Barbara swept her teeth with her tongue to keep from smiling. It seemed forever before Lila came into the dining room, carrying a tray of salads, which she served speedily before she retreated into the kitchen. Looking down at the creation in her china salad bowl, Barbara could understand why the hasty retreat was necessary. Never had she put her eyes upon a more pitiful offering of wilted lettuce and overripe tomatoes. And it was anybody's guess what kind of dressing Lila had splattered on top of it. After seeing her two employers attack their bowls with apparent hearty appetites, she reluctantly reached for her salad fork. Glaring at her food, she was unsure of what to do. It was obvious to her that food preparation was not Lila's strong point.

Slightly past seven, when the meal was finished, Henrietta suggested they all meet outside on the terrace in thirty minutes to begin their project. Barbara then excused herself from the dining room to walk outside and seconds later stood on the porch, viewing her surroundings. The sun was sinking low in the west behind a cluster of tall pines. A thoughtful expression on her face, she walked down the steps onto the drive, trying to relax her stomach. She felt somewhat anxious about the work which would commence in a few minutes. As she walked, the muscles in her legs seemed with each step to constrict instead of to relax. She moved from the drive onto a stone path, which eventually led

33

around to the west side of the house after weaving in and out among tall old trees. The sound of a car motor brought her to a half turn to see John Michael drive up in front of the house and get out of his car. To her surprise he was alone, and she watched from the pathway as he bounded up the steps and ran across the wide porch to enter the house.

Breathing in the pure evening air, Barbara sighed and casually continued her walk. *How smart was it to come here, Barbara Whitney?* she asked herself over and over again. She lingered among the trees for several long moments, one hand reaching out to touch the rough bark of a tremendous oak, a tree probably older than the lovely old house. She glanced at her watch and was about to turn in the direction of the house when a deep voice sounded behind her.

"Out for a walk, Miss Whitney?"

Barbara wheeled about to face John Michael Stewart. "Yes," she answered bluntly, wondering how he had sneaked so close without her hearing his footsteps. "It's a lovely evening," she added almost as an afterthought.

He gazed at her quite searchingly. Then he smiled. "Have you had dinner?"

"Yes."

"And are you settled in?"

She nodded, saying, "For the most part." She couldn't stop herself from thinking John Michael Stewart was an extremely handsome man, perhaps as handsome as any man she had ever seen.

They walked side by side along the path, and from the corner of her eyes she took note of the way he carried himself, of the self-assurance in his steps, his posture, the manner in which his clothes fitted. It was plain he was a man with his rightful share of self-confidence.

He took a deep breath of the still, warm air, then asked, "Doesn't your conscience bother you at all?" He glanced at her and smiled.

Caught somewhat off guard by the question which accompanied the smile, she answered, "Should it?"

He shrugged. "I don't know, but I think mine probably would."

She didn't particularly care for the drift of this conversation and immediately recognized his tactic. "Then perhaps your conscience knows something mine doesn't," she replied calmly as her brilliant blue eyes flashed at him. She wouldn't let him make her feel guilty, not now, not ever. She had simply answered an advertisement.

"Yes," he continued, "I believe I would feel quite bad about taking advantage of two elderly ladies. We both know, Miss Whitney, that the chances of any measure of success in this venture are practically nil. Why, you could write a book about what they don't know about writing."

Barbara frowned. "We'll see, Mr. Stewart." She was determined not to let him influence her decision. She was here, and here she would stay until she decided to leave. The decision would be dictated by her emotions, not by someone else, least of all a self-serving nephew obviously out to protect his own interest. She glared at him for an instant; then her eyes dropped. The tension between them was becoming unbearable.

"I merely want you to be reasonable," he said, reaching one hand out in the direction of her arm.

Barbara edged backward to avoid his touch. Tossing her head, she said, "I *am* being reasonable, Mr. Stewart. I was hired to do a job, and that's exactly what I intend to do. For me to do otherwise would be unreasonable."

He folded his arms across his chest. "Then you're determined?" he asked.

"Yes, I'm afraid so."

A faint smile swept across his lips, but his eyes remained on her. Then, without another word to her, he turned and walked back toward the house, his lips pursed in utmost concentration.

When Barbara reached the terrace, she found the two women waiting for her. "Just let me rush upstairs and get my tape recorder," she announced pleasantly, "and I'll be with you."

"Oh, no, dear," Hannah said softly, "I'm afraid we couldn't do that."

"Oh, no," Henrietta joined in, "not a tape recorder. We just wouldn't be natural speaking into one of those things."

Barbara nodded and stepped toward the door. "Then I'll get my note pad and pen," she finally said, attempting to cover her disappointment. She glanced over her shoulder at the darkening sky and wondered if they expected her to take notes in the dark.

Just as she reached for the door, it opened, and John Michael stepped out and pulled the doors closed behind him, holding fast to the knobs. "It's a lovely evening, isn't it?" he said, first looking at his aunts, then bestowing a toothy smile at Barbara.

Both women looked up at him and smiled, but the happy lights in their eyes dulled. Barbara stood back with a watchful expression on her face.

"You don't mind if I join you, do you?" he inquired softly, pleasantly. "I can't think of a better way to spend time than with my two favorite aunts." He hesitated and added sweetly, "And their guest, of course."

Hannah looked swiftly at her sister's prim face and both sets of eyes widened. After a moment she asked, "You don't have any work to do tonight?"

He laughed. "Nothing that can't wait until tomorrow." Slowly his hands slid away from the doors, and his thumbs caught on the back pockets of the jeans he'd put on since entering the house. "I was just thinking how nice it would be if we all had a glass of wine and got to know Miss Whitney a little better. I know you don't intend for her to work tonight, not after the long trip she's made to be here."

Henrietta swallowed and glanced first at her sister, then over at Barbara. "Of course, we don't," she uttered in a low voice. "We were just sitting out here enjoying the sunset together."

Still wearing his generous smile, he said, "Let me go inside and pour the wine." Then he turned to Barbara. "Would you care to come with me, Miss Whitney?"

Barbara looked at him, her lips pursed. "I'd be happy to, Mr. Stewart," she replied coolly.

Turning, he held the doors open for her. She entered first, and he followed close behind, so close, in fact, that she could feel his breath on her neck.

"In the living room," he stated matter-of-factly, the laughter suddenly gone from his voice. As they walked silently down the hallway, she could feel his eyes staring into the back of her head.

When the door to the living room creaked loudly, she was startled to look around and see that he had closed it. She glanced sharply at him. Silent and preoccupied, he moved across the room and placed four glasses on a tray. Barbara's eyes left him momentarily as she again scanned the room and its furnishings, astonished by its sheer loveliness.

She was standing with her back to the door, and hearing it creak again, she looked around to see Lila stick her head inside. "John Michael," the woman said solemnly, "can you take me to the doctor's office tomorrow?"

Pouring the wine, John Michael glanced around. "I have court tomorrow, Lila. What about Friday?"

"I don't think I can wait until Friday."

John Michael looked at Barbara, a question in his blue eyes. "Miss Whitney, do you suppose you could drive Lila in to see the doctor tomorrow? I would, but as I explained, I have to be in court."

Barbara, caught off guard, stammered, "I-I don't know. I'd have to check with—"

"No"—he interrupted with assuredness—"it's all right. Believe me, Lila's health is more important to my aunts than anything else. I would appreciate it if you would."

"Well." Barbara felt trapped, not knowing exactly what to say. "I suppose . . ." Her words trailed off.

Lila gave her a harried smile. "I'll be ready about eight-thirty."

"That early?" Barbara said with some surprise. She never knew of a doctor's opening his office at eight-thirty, but perhaps the South was different.

When the door closed, John Michael lifted the silver tray bearing four glasses from the marble-topped table and turned, raising his brows at her. "I really appreciate your doing this, Miss Whitney. We try to make Lila feel like one of the family in these little ways. I don't know what my aunts would do without her."

Probably put on a little weight, Barbara thought, but said nothing.

"Ready?" he said, walking over with the tray in his hands, giving her a most pleasant smile.

Her penetrating blue eyes regarded him for a long moment.

With a much too amiable expression on his good-looking face he moved with catlike grace to the door and paused, waiting for her to open it for him.

Almost under her breath she said quietly as she approached the door, "For some reason I don't trust you, Mr. Stewart."

Turning his head, he grinned at her. "In that case, why don't you call me John?"

Grim-faced, she followed him back out onto the terrace, where the two women sat waiting patiently for their nephew to serve the wine. Barbara stood back, watching him, looking at the back of his muscular body, unable to keep from wondering where his wife was at this moment.

"Guess what?" he announced briskly. "Miss Whitney has kindly volunteered to drive Lila to the doctor in the morning. Wasn't that kind of her?"

The two women immediately glanced at each other. "Oh, dear." Henrietta's voice quivered as she whispered the two words. Hannah, unable to mask her disappointment, sat staring mutely at her nephew.

When everyone held a glass, John Michael laughed and slyly winked at Barbara. "Let us toast," he said with exaggerated enthusiasm, "our one big happy family."

Both wearing disheartened expressions, Henrietta and Hannah Stewart slowly raised their glasses. It was obvious to Barbara that John Michael Stewart had become much too happy over nothing. But on second thought perhaps it was something after all. He had skillfully managed to delay the start of his aunts' project for another few hours.

Henrietta sipped her wine; then, as she lowered her glass away from her mouth, she looked at her nephew and questioned, "Who's looking after your place, son?"

"Spence," he replied, clearing his throat. "The crops are all planted, so it's a quiet time with just the cattle and horses to look after. He won't be overworked."

A couple of hours later Barbara, sitting upstairs in her bedroom, brushing her hair, thoughtfully retraced much of the conversation which had taken place outside. It seemed terribly strange to her that at no time had John Michael's wife been mentioned. Very probably, Barbara finally concluded, he was divorced.

CHAPTER THREE

By three o'clock the next afternoon Barbara felt sure that John Michael Stewart was indeed a divorced man and even had an inkling why. What woman with a good mind would put up with a sneaky, conniving man in today's world? She'd certainly been had, and in a big way, with Lila and her doctor deal.

Disgusted enough to die as she baked under the hot southern sun, Barbara felt as if the day were endless. From the five o'clock tap on her door before daybreak to inform her breakfast was ready until this moment, as she sat in the parking lot of the pharmacy at Corinth, thirty miles north of Baldwyn, the day had been a nightmare. John Michael Stewart had negligently failed to mention the fact that Lila's physician was located thirty miles from the Stewart home, plus the fact that the doctor didn't make appointments. It was first come, first serve. Barbara had been aghast to see the line of patients waiting outside the door when she and Lila first arrived at the small brick clinic. Lila must have become patient number fifty at least. Of course, there had not been sufficient room inside the air-conditioned building for Barbara, so she had been forced to broil outside. Her frustration with the man responsible was the only motivation she had going for her at the present time.

Hours ago, after leaving for the doctor's office, Lila had mentioned something about suffering from "raw nerves." Glancing often toward the pharmacy door, Barbara was beginning to feel the same symptoms. She thought of all the things she might have accomplished today, but thanks to the nephew, it had been a futile, trying day.

At four-thirty in the afternoon the homeward trip began. Lila sat clutching the white pharmacy bag in her lap, staring out the window. Following a prolonged silence, Barbara glanced over and said, "Are you feeling better?"

Lila nodded and said, "Some."

A few miles down the busy highway Barbara questioned, "Does John Michael usually drive you to the doctor's office?" She couldn't believe for a moment a busy attorney would take a full day from work to chauffeur his aunts' maid around.

"Most of the time, but if he's tied up in court,

then he usually sends someone from the office to drive me."

"Really." Barbara's voice dropped to a whisper as she tried to hide her annoyance.

"He's a fine, thoughtful man," Lila suddenly declared strongly. "If he had his way, I tell you the prisons in this state would be empty. He believes there's good in everyone." She sniffed, then asked bluntly, "Do you have a favorite dessert? If you do, I'll make it for you tonight."

"Thanks, but I rarely eat sweets," Barbara replied quietly. A feeling of guilt clouded her heart. Could it be that she had been silently blasting an innocent man all day long? She glanced at Lila. "How well do you know the Stewarts?"

"Pretty good. But there's not many Stewarts left. Just three or four, I think."

Barbara's eyes traveled quickly back to the road. Taking a deep breath, she asked straight out, "Is Mr. Stewart divorced?"

Lila's mouth opened wide. "Why, goodness, no. What makes you ask such a question?"

Awkwardly Barbara replied, "Miss Henrietta mentioned his wife at one time."

"Oh," Lila said, then lapsed into silence.

Barbara waited for Lila to say more and, when she didn't, looked to see the woman again staring out the window. Barbara grimaced slightly, then lapsed into silence, withdrawing within herself and becoming preoccupied for a distance with thoughts of home and other things. On the outskirts of Baldwyn she looked again at Lila and said, "Why do I get the feeling there's something ominous about the subject of John Michael's wife? Is there a mystery, Lila?"

"I don't think so," Lila said, and added after a moment, "Actually she wasn't his wife. I don't know the exact arrangement, but I do know they weren't married. He brought her here to meet his aunts, and from what I've been able to piece together, John Michael and the woman must have shared the same bedroom." After a short hesitation Lila went on. "Now that didn't set well with the ladies of the house, so they started calling her John Michael's wife. But as far as I know, they never did get married."

Brows raised, Barbara said, "Oh, really?" She already had a clue to which bedroom they had shared.

"Anyway, by the time summer ended the woman took an itch to leave, and I think John Michael was glad she did. However, by that time the ladies had told so many folks that they were married it set tongues to wagging pretty good. Matter of fact, I suppose I'm one of the few who know that they never were married. It caused a big to-do between him and his aunts." She looked sharply at Barbara. "It never pays to get mixed up with someone from some other part of the country. Folks should stick to their own kind."

46

For a moment Barbara drove on in silence. Then she asked quietly, "Where was she from?"

"I don't know for sure, but from somewhere up North, Connecticut or Delaware. It was one of those little states with a big name." Lila opened the pharmacy bag and held up a bottle of capsules. "Do you know that this bottle of medicine has gone up over two dollars since the last time I had it filled? Now isn't that a crying shame!"

Barbara nodded, then sighed in relief at seeing the WELCOME TO BALDWYN sign. Glancing at her watch, she gave a little shake of her head. Ten minutes to five. Perhaps there was still time to accomplish a little before the ladies' eight o'clock bedtime.

Then Lila said, "If you don't mind, I need to stop by the grocery store and pick up a few things."

At exactly six-thirty Barbara, along with Lila and a car packed full of groceries, pulled onto the Stewart drive, then around to the rear of the house so she could help Lila unload the groceries.

Finally she went up to her room and fell in an exhausted heap into the antique rocker. Slowly she began to rock back and forth, pursing, then relaxing her lips. She absolutely refused to become a pawn in John Stewart's attempt to thwart his aunts' ambitions. With a somewhat mournful expression on her face she massaged

47

her temples. What in this world had she gotten herself into? When a tap sounded at the door, she dropped her hands, turned, and said, "Yes?"

Slowly the door opened and a grinning John Michael strolled into her bedroom. "Hello," he said cheerfully.

"Umph," she grunted, eyeing him with solemnity.

"Have a good day?"

It was obvious to Barbara he was having too much fun at her expense. There was a silence for a few seconds before she replied coolly, "A most satisfactory day. Thank you for giving me the opportunity to see more of this area."

"Oh, you're more than welcome." He laughed, then unable to keep from teasing her more, added, "Lila gets her hormone shots once a month. If you're still here next month, you can do this again since you found it to be such a pleasant experience. But you've seen only a small part of the area. Did you know you passed by the highest mountain in the state? Maybe next trip you can stop and get a closer look."

She, of course, picked up on the sneaky way he had said, "If you're still here next month," but let it slide since he seemed to be enjoying himself to such an extent. In a level tone she replied, "I didn't see anything that even slightly resembled a mountain." Her eyes rested solidly on his face.

Still smiling with pleasure, he said, "Maybe

after dinner we could drive out. It helps digest one of Lila's meals when you climb a small mountain."

A hint of caution slipped across piercing blue eyes. Now what kind of game was he playing? "Thank you," she said, countering his invitation smoothly, "but I'm sure your aunts will have work for me after dinner."

"Oh, I don't think so," he said with such sureness Barbara's eyes widened. Then he inquired, "You didn't by chance see them when you and Lila finally returned from your day's excursion, did you?"

"No." She hadn't seen the ladies, but she'd come straight from the kitchen upstairs.

"This is Wednesday, Miss Whitney. They always leave for church promptly at six on Wednesday evening, and they won't be home until nine or so. They won't be working, if you can call it that, on Sundays or Wednesdays." His smile widened. "They have a very strict routine, one which you'll have to work around."

Barbara replied sweetly, "I'm sure that I'll manage. I'm usually very adaptable to my circumstances."

"That's good to know." His eyes caught and held hers. Smiling, he added, "I'll remember that in the days to come." There was a short silence, and then, half turning to the door, he said, "Lila will have dinner ready about seven-thirty."

"Thank you. I'll be down." She tossed her head cockily. After the door had closed behind him, Barbara looked around the room somewhat absently, her face still a solemn mask. Then she shook her head as if to clear away her thoughts. She had taken on a big enough challenge without adding another. John Michael Stewart was a handsome, masculine, dashing man, but he was also something more, something she couldn't quite put her finger on. Whatever it was, Barbara felt she had best ignore it.

After rising from the rocker, she walked to the closet and removed freshly laundered jeans and a short-sleeved sweater from hangers, subconsciously preparing herself to climb a mountain after dinner if the invitation was repeated. After a quick bath she went down the stairs at exactly seven-thirty. Entering the dining room, she saw John lean back in the chair at the head of the table.

Barbara moved toward her chair in quick steps, shifting her gaze away from John Michael's face. He rose to his feet and waited for her to be seated, watching her intently all the time. He continued standing for a moment, and his mouth curved in a slow smile as he looked down at her. "Would you like a drink before dinner?" he asked in a low voice.

Unwilling to meet his eyes, she answered softly, "No, thank you," very much perturbed with herself for the awkward little feeling playing inside her chest. She'd never been one to allow a man's gaze to set her off-balance, and she had no intention of starting now.

Reseating himself, John Michael remarked casually, "Tell me, Barbara, have you formed an impression of our part of the world?"

She lifted her eyes to meet his and replied without hesitation, "I'm not one to form quick opinions." He had called her Barbara, not Miss Whitney. Already the barriers were coming down, or so he must think.

The trip to the doctor's office had visibly improved Lila's disposition, but not her culinary skills. She came breezing into the room, humming under her breath, holding a platter of something unidentifiable in her hands. "I didn't fix much," she announced pleasantly, "since the ladies aren't here." She placed the platter midway between the two diners and stepped back, resting her hands at her sides.

John shifted his gaze swiftly to Barbara, then back to the platter. "Ummm, french fries and uh . . ." Suddenly smiling, he said abruptly, "Looks good." After Lila had disappeared back into the kitchen, still humming, he laughed softly and tilted his head toward Barbara. "I think that's chicken beside the potatoes, but I wasn't sure, so when in doubt, especially with Lila's meals, it's best to change the subject."

Barbara smiled easily, eyeing the platter. "I

think I see something that vaguely resembles a drumstick."

"Both my aunts have tried to convince Lila to buy chickens that are already cut up, but she insists that they cost too much, so she buys them whole and then dismembers them into the weirdest pieces." He gestured at her. "Go ahead, help yourself. Take your pick."

"All right," Barbara laughed jovially. "I think I'll take this 'threast.' It looks like a cross between a thigh and a breast." Chuckling under her breath, she took the piece of meat.

He sat looking at her, waiting until she replaced the serving fork before he said with a darting, flirtatious glance, "You have a nice laugh, Barbara."

She looked at him, acknowledging his words with a fleeting smile but saying nothing. Then she turned her attention to the meal.

Watching her closely, he smiled, then turned his own attention to his plate. They ate in silence. Finally pushing himself from the table and dangling one arm across the back of his chair, John Michael gazed at her in silence. He pursed his lips for a brief moment before saying, "Are you this quiet in New Jersey?"

"Rarely," she replied behind the napkin raised to her lips. "I am one of a large family, and it's usually anything but quiet."

"Oh." He seemed surprised. "Do you live at home?"

She gave one quick shake of her head. "No, but I visit frequently."

"And you teach school?"

"Yes. High school English."

He rubbed his chin thoughtfully as he examined her face. Then, with a genuine smile, he admitted, "I never had a teacher who looked like you." He stared at her speculatively. "I'm sure you look as youthful as many of your students."

"Only when I'm out of the classroom," she replied pleasantly. "In the classroom setting the age difference is very noticeable, believe me."

Looking relaxed and comfortable, he continued to stare at her. She realized she still felt a little nervous in his presence. Another minute passed, and she began haltingly to rise from her chair. "If you'll excuse me, I think I'll go upstairs."

He stood when she did. "Does that mean you don't want to see the mountain? I thought maybe you did." His eyes swept across her attire, then back to her face.

She shook her head quickly and said, "No, I think I'll get a good night's rest and be ready for tomorrow. I feel certain we'll begin work in the morning." She approached the doorway leading out to the hall.

Suddenly he reached past her, halting her abruptly so that she found herself pinned between his body and his outstretched arm. "I think it's only fair to warn you at the onset, Barbara, I will do everything in my power to cripple this so-called project of my aunts."

"I don't doubt that," she answered. "Good night, John Michael."

In the next second she was turned around and in his arms. He pulled her closer and, holding her chin firmly, forced her gaze to meet his. His lips parted, and he said, "That is not to say that your visit South couldn't be enjoyable and educational nonetheless."

She closed her eyes and tried to pull free of his grasp, choking out the words. "It seems to me you assume a great deal, Mr. Stewart, and I resent this highly irregular approach to try changing my mind."

He smiled as his brows rose, and he brought his face so close to hers that their noses brushed. "I have this feeling you'll change your mind—in time."

She needed breathing space. Opening her hands against his shirt, she pressed firmly against his chest to push him back. The closeness of his body, his face gave rise in her to a mixture of emotions, not the least of which was anger. Still, her mind was very clear regarding the best strategy for this particular situation. Slowly her eyes opened wide, her long lashes almost touching his cheek. He wanted to play kissing games. A grown man, an attorney, actually believed he could sway her judgment with lip trivia. She had never been one to back away from a challenge. Her hands stopped pressing him away, and the moment his lips touched hers, she returned the kiss in measure. Her lips were parted, her eyelids half hiding fiery, glowing eyes. His lids closed; his arms tightened about her as his mouth moved against her in a savoring caress. Barbara found herself ill-prepared for the sudden ringing in her ears, the rapid beat of her heart as his mouth pressed harder against hers.

A low "Oh, dear," from the hallway made them jump apart, and Barbara heard her own gasp. Both she and John turned at the same time to see the two ladies standing in the hallway, shock and bewilderment on their faces. Barbara knew without doubt she was facing the greatest moment of embarrassment in her life.

"John Michael," Henrietta declared with despair in her voice, "what do you think you're doing?"

"Yes." Hannah joined in, equally perturbed. "Is that any way to treat our guest?"

John smiled with smooth assurance at the two elderly faces, and when he spoke, there was a hint of laughter, teasing in his voice, a twinkle in his eyes. "You're home early, aren't you?"

"Lucky for Miss Whitney, I daresay," Henrietta snapped.

Barbara felt herself caught in the crossfire as she stood smiling bleakly at the two women. Still, she could find a certain pleasure in the ladies' taking their nephew to task. In seconds Barbara's expression had changed from one of pure embarrassment to one of utmost innocence.

"I'm afraid you've both jumped to the wrong conclusion," John said simply. "I was only telling Miss Whitney good night."

The two women exchanged questioning looks. Then Hannah turned to John, stating bluntly, "Well, if you've quite finished saying good night, Henrietta and I would like a few minutes with Miss Whitney."

His hands slid into his pockets, and he grinned sheepishly at the two women. After strolling casually to the stairway, he hesitated and glanced around at his aunts. "Oh, by the way, I may be driving down to Vicksburg tomorrow to interview a potential witness for my next court case. I thought maybe the two of you would like to come along and visit with Uncle Harold. After all, he's not getting any younger."

Barbara propped her shoulder against the door frame and watched the exchange taking place. Hannah sighed first and shook her head while John Michael stood and waited patiently for his offer to take the desired effect. At length Henrietta said, "I just don't see how we can . . ." Her words trailed off, and she looked helplessly at her sister for alliance.

"No." Hannah joined in after a brief pause. "We're not getting any younger ourselves, and unless we begin our project with Miss Whitney, the summer will be over and she'll be gone."

Henrietta interrupted with "Besides, the last time we visited Harold, he called us two geese in search of a gander, and neither of us considered that a very gracious remark. He's never understood our choices in life, and I see no reason to make a long trip in order to visit a man who delights in belittling us. I think Christmas will be soon enough to visit Harold."

"I agree," Hannah said. "Christmas will be quite soon enough."

John Michael reached up and raked one hand through his hair. "I didn't say I would definitely be making the trip," he said quietly. Then, as he looked at his aunts, his mouth settled into a firm, resolute line.

Barbara stood absorbing the encounter. She knew exactly what John Michael was up to with the spur-of-the-moment trip. But why? Perhaps the explanation he'd offered yesterday had been a smoke screen to camouflage the real reason he opposed the Stewart sisters' project. She was sure the legal implications bore some truth, but now she had the feeling that it was much more than some obscure fear of a court battle. It was almost as if he were trying to hide something or perhaps to protect something or maybe someone. What? Whom? Her curiosity heightened as she watched him climb the stairs.

When he reached the second level, he hesitated and looked down at her. Their eyes met for a moment. Then he looked away and stepped off down the hallway. Barbara moved from the dining room doorway and stepped directly in front of the two women, both now wearing long, drawn expressions.

Henrietta shrugged. "I refuse to feel guilty about not going to see Harold," she stated flatly.

Hannah nodded in agreement, then added the question "Don't you agree, Miss Whitney?"

Barbara smiled thinly. "Is he your brother?"

"No," Henrietta answered. "He's our father's younger brother. He's ninety-four years old and as cantankerous as he was at fifty. He could have stayed up here where he'd be close to family, what little's left, but no, he had to get himself admitted to a veterans' rest home clear at the other end of the state. And do you know why?" Her eyes widened, growing large and round. "Because he likes nurses. In his ninety-four years he's been in and out of every VA hospital in the central states, winking and blinking and acting a fool in general. Why, the last time we visited him, he spoke most unkindly about the two of us, and that old goat was sitting there with his bottom dentures in upside down, which was a sight within itself. Then in mid-sentence he took off in his wheelchair, racing down the corridor after the day nurse. It was disgusting to think a Stewart could behave so ungentlemanly."

58

"Was he a hero or anything like that?" Barbara laughed softly.

"A hero!" Hannah laughed. "Goodness, no. He only served a few weeks near the close of the First World War, and believe me, Uncle Sam has paid dearly for those few days of service. The truth is, he got a hernia from lifting a bag of potatoes when he was on KP. He said it kept him from having a normal life, and I guess it did because as far as I know he's never lifted another thing since then."

"He didn't get the hernia repaired?" Barbara asked, shocked.

Henrietta shook her head in dismay. "No. That hernia was his Medal of Honor, and he's worn it proudly for nearly seventy years." Suddenly she paused, taking a deep breath. "But enough about Harold. What my sister and I wanted to discuss with you is the beginning of our book."

"Oh." Barbara smiled, encouraged. It was much too early to consider going to bed.

"Yes." Hannah sighed. "But after the deal about Harold I'm much too tired to begin tonight. Why don't we just make plans to begin early in the morning?" She glanced at her sister. "Is that satisfactory with you, Henrietta?"

"Oh, yes, tomorrow will be fine." She passed a hand limply across her forehead. "We should never begin anything following a conversation

59

about Harold Stewart. I agree we all retire and begin anew tomorrow."

Half an hour later Barbara stood in her room, her face a mask of confusion. Slowly she walked over to the heavy drapes and pulled one back to peer out at the night. Moonlight flooded through the tall trees, reaching across the lawn with a mellow veil of light but leaving corners and shadows hidden in darkness. She tried not to think about the brief encounter downstairs with John Michael, but it was on her mind, moving slowly across her thoughts. "You're up to something," she said aloud, "but you'll soon find I won't be a pawn in a game between you and your aunts."

After a few moments she looked away from the window and over at the bed. Her sigh was deep and thoughtful when she heard a soft tap on her door. She crossed the room, knowing full well who was standing outside the door. She paused for several moments with her hand on the knob before opening it to see John standing in the hallway.

After a long moment of silence he asked, "May I come in?"

Barbara looked down at the floor. "I don't know why you're bothering," she said, pushing a loose strand of dark hair from her eyes. "I'm not your problem," she stated bluntly, raising her eyes back toward him.

He looked at her straight on, his probing eyes

making her feel uncomfortable. He smiled, propping himself against the door frame, crossing his arms over his chest. He was really a good-looking man in all the best ways: a smooth, handsome face, open and honest, an ideal face for an attorney.

"I don't consider you a problem, Barbara. My hope is that we might strike a resolution that could be beneficial to both of us. I have real doubts that you have any inkling of what lies in store for you in the days ahead."

Her brows rose. "And I'll never know if you persist in placing obstacles in the path."

He stared at her innocently, repeating, "May I come in?"

Stepping back, Barbara opened the door wider, muttering, "I don't think your aunts would approve."

Darting a glance at her, John Michael allowed the remark to pass unanswered. After taking the door from her hand, he closed it softly behind him, then leaned against it, a near frown wrinkling his smooth brow. Under his steady gaze Barbara felt a certain discomfort with his presence in the room. "Do you mind if we talk awhile?" he asked, leaning forward toward her.

She gave a single shake of her head. "I suppose not."

He said nothing for a moment, as if undecided exactly what he intended to say, and Barbara felt sure she was seeing his jury summation face.

61

Then he said in a straightforward voice, "I suppose you think I'm making much ado about nothing."

She remained silent, still not comfortable with the way he was staring at her.

"I'm just so opposed to this whole thing," he added, then paused again.

"Why don't you give it some time?" she suggested softly. "It's been said millions of people start books but relatively few complete them. Why don't you allow us to begin without any more interruptions and see what happens?"

"But you see"—his voice dropped to little more than a whisper—"I know Stewarts are a determined brood, and there isn't a doubt in my mind that barring unforeseen complications, my aunts will do precisely what they intend."

"And would that be so terrible, considering at that point the true obstacles begin?" She momentarily turned her eyes from him, a melancholy smile on her lips. "Why not just allow nature its course?"

He fell silent for a moment and looked at her searchingly. "I'll tell you what," he said after a while. "I won't interfere any further if you will promise to keep me informed of the story line as it unfolds."

The request surprised her. Her blue eyes caught his and held. "Why?" she asked bluntly.

He smiled easily and tilted his head questioningly at her. "I can be using my spare time to begin preparing my future briefs," he said evasively, then grinned and added, "No, seriously, I, uh, am interested in the selection of happenings my aunts feel—"

Barbara glared at him, her arms folding slowly across her chest. "What are you afraid of, John?" Suddenly she laughed. "Are you afraid you'll be a lead character? Perhaps something about the romantic escapades of John Michael Stewart?"

"No." He huffed emphatically. "No, I'm not."

She answered quickly, "Well, don't try to convince me it's this lawyer thing, some obscure fear of future suits. I just don't buy that at all, not one word of it."

"Well, what would you buy?" he queried in a gentle voice.

"I don't know."

He shook his head from side to side, then chuckled. "I see the teacher in you."

"Just as I see your feeble excuses for what they are," she said comfortably.

He held up one finger in warning. "I want you to remember this conversation, Miss Whitney. Remember the night I came to your room in an attempt to reason with you."

"I'll remember," she said glibly with a quick smile.

He gave a little shake of his head. "I have this very distinct feeling that Hannah and Henrietta Stewart couldn't have searched the world over and found a more faithful coconspirator."

63

For a moment she stood mesmerized by the expressive look on his face. Then slowly she felt the smile fading from her lips. Self-consciously she cast her eyes down. "It's getting late. I suppose you need to go if you've finished with your plea bargaining."

His gaze followed her as she moved in a path around him close to the door. "I also came to apologize for what happened downstairs. I didn't mean to place you in an embarrassing situation."

She shrugged with total composure. "No reason to apologize. Your aunts credited you one hundred percent with the event."

He laughed, then said teasingly, "Of course, I should have realized that they would see you as an innocent, completely at the mercy of long-armed John."

"Wasn't I?"

With narrowed eyes he chuckled. "It was nothing that required mercy, simply the action of impulse, Barbara."

She stood face-to-face with him, and for a moment their eyes locked before she looked away. "You'll soon discover I'm not an impulsive person," she said lightly.

He reached out to take one of her hands and held it between his. "You're a very attractive woman, but you already know that, don't you?"

She tried to sound flippant as she slipped her

hand from his. "I've never noticed the mirror being overly kind to me."

"And modest." He laughed good-naturedly. "Not impulsive and modest, two commendable characteristics."

"Don't start a file on me."

Opening the door, he said chidingly, "Too late. The moment you joined in with that pair downstairs you gave me no choice but to begin my defense." Suddenly he hesitated, and he looked around the room. Then stepping out into the hallway, he said softly, "Good night, ghost-writer."

"Good night," she replied. After slowly closing the door, she leaned back against it and listened as his footsteps echoed down the hallway, then thudded loudly down the stairway. *That man,* she thought, feeling suddenly horrified, *he'll announce to everyone in this house he's been upstairs in my room.* Then she grimaced, wondering if that had been his intention.

CHAPTER FOUR

When noon arrived the next day, Barbara found
herself saying under her breath, "Thank goodness!" It had been a morning like none other in
her life. The lengthy session with the two elderly ladies had developed into nothing short of
a waking nightmare. Looking at the note pad in
her hand with an expression of helplessness, she
wondered what in the world she would be expected to do with the muddled mess of words
she had scribbled almost nonstop in spite of the
numerous arguments which had erupted between the two dictating parties, who now sat
staring at each other indignantly. More than a
little uncomfortable with the dampening atmo-
sphere, Barbara busied herself with turning
back through the pages and glancing helplessly
at the notes.

"What do you think, dear?" Henrietta asked
in a tone of dismay.

Positioning the note pad on her legs and placing her hands lightly on top of it, Barbara sought for diplomacy in her reply. "Uh . . ." She tilted her head. "I'm not sure."

Hannah Stewart gave her sister a look of fury. "And just what do you think she thinks, Henrietta? She thinks it's a mess, which it is! I can't believe after all our discussions you have hogged the entire morning with your long-winded tales which amount to less than a hill of beans. I will absolutely refuse to put my name on or be associated with anything so simpleminded as the stories you've suggested this morning! I thought we had agreed to give the world a work of importance, something significant about small-town life."

"And just what do you think I've been doing all morning, Hannah?" Henrietta replied with equal fury. "While you've been sitting there, pursing your lips, hoping for just the right words to jump out, I've been laying the groundwork. I merely suggested a few incidents."

"Which have absolutely nothing to do with one another!" Hannah interrupted with far too much sweetness in her voice. "What you have done is waste the morning for the three of us, dear sister. I daresay there is not a person alive who cares about Joe Rainey's pig farm, which could be whiffed five miles away." She hesitated. "Or Etta Wilson's mysterious visitor sixty-five years ago, because it's still a mystery! We don't know who the man was or why he visited poor, plain Etta in the first place. The only certain fact that came out of that encounter was the child born that summer, and you didn't even bother to tell Miss Whitney about that event because you had already switched to that long tale about how the railroad company bypassed our town in the late 1800s with its precious depot." Not taking her gaze from her sister's face, Hannah stopped talking.

Barbara raised one hand in slow motion and rubbed one eye. Then, solemn-faced, she looked from one sulking woman to the other sulking woman. After a searching pause she said in a very low voice, "You know, ladies, what I had hoped for this morning was an outline of the story you have in mind. An outline is a very useful tool in writing because it sets a course for us to follow." Seeing the downcast expression on Henrietta's face, she became even more gentle with her words. "That's not to say that the stories this morning weren't interesting. It's merely that they weren't really connected to each other."

At that precise moment Lila stuck her head in the room and announced, "Your lunch is getting cold!" She then added, "And if you're planning on changing your lunchtime, you need to let me know 'cause I ain't no mind reader."

"Oh, dear." Hannah sighed. "I didn't realize it

was so late. Now Lila's got herself in a stew."
Sweetly she called, "We'll be right there, Lila."

"I'm not hungry in the least," Henrietta whispered weakly. "You and Miss Whitney go ahead and eat. Don't worry about me," she added in an anguished tone of voice.

Barbara and Hannah left the room with Henrietta remaining behind, huddled in her chair, looking as if she'd lost the last friend she had in the world.

Needless to say, Lila's cold french fries and greasy salmon patties left something to be desired, and Barbara merely sat rolling her eyes helplessly when Hannah excused herself from the table, holding her forehead, laying claim to a sudden headache. Halting at the door, she looked back unhappily and said, "You and Henrietta continue on without me, dear. I don't feel I'd be of much use this afternoon."

After a much needed walk around the front lawn and along the trail weaving in and out among the tall pines, Barbara returned to the house and started back into the parlor, where she expected to find Henrietta. Instead, she found an empty room. She lifted her note pad from the table and left the room, thinking she would spend the afternoon sorting through the notes in an attempt to put some order into the morning's work. She agreed with Hannah that Joe Rainey's pig farm was of little interest, and the railroad's decision to place the depot twenty miles away would at this point have dubious effect on the story, but the Etta Wilson section of the notes could perhaps bear closer scrutiny. There was something of an intrigue there, or perhaps there could be if the idea were properly developed.

Upon entering her office, she sat down at the desk and opened the notebook, only to discover the entire morning's notes had been ripped out. Leaning forward over the desk, she caught her head in both hands and moaned aloud. "Oh, no, Henrietta Stewart, what did you do that for?" Her fingers buried themselves in her curly brown hair. If there was any truth in the old saying "A bad beginning makes a good ending," she was in for one bang-up finish.

Sighing aloud, she straightened and began to look at the books on the desk. She might as well find something to do to occupy the remaining hours of the afternoon, for she knew with a certainty work on the Stewart sisters' masterpiece was ended for the day. Finally deciding on an Emilie Loring novel, she removed it from the neat arrangement stacked between two antique bookends. Then she left the room and almost crept through the deadly silent house, back down the stairs and out the door. Walking around to the side, she deliberated about settling down on the terrace, but the large oak tree which stood in solitude beyond the narrow gap in the hedge looked inviting, and without conscious thought she slipped down the path and through the hedge. Moments later she was settled comfortably beneath the tree, her back against the trunk, her eyes resting on the full leafy boughs above her head. Clutching the book to her chest, she folded her arms across it, her mind taking in the majestic silence, the strange peacefulness she felt sweeping over her. It had been years since she had sat under a tree. Sitting with silence all around and looking at the blades of grass, the blueness of the sky, hearing the soft rustle of the green leaves being swept by a quiet late-spring breeze, made her almost feel as if the soft arms of nature were enwrapping her bodily. How many days and months and years had she walked through life unconscious of these elements, which were in themselves life-giving? Slowly breathing in the air of sweet-scented pines, of fresh-blooming roses, she let her eyes rest on tender green leaves, and felt an inner wistfulness without analyzing the source.

Barbara sat there beneath the tree, reading and enjoying the outdoors until midafternoon, when she glanced up and saw John Michael standing near the hedge, peering over at her. She did not speak at once, but she felt her lips part in surprise.

"Hello," he said, grinning, looking into her eyes. "I understand the morning didn't go well with the Hemingway sisters."

"True," she replied sprightly. "And does that make you happy?"

He laughed and shook his head. "I don't know that *happy* is the right word, but I am a bit relieved." As he started moving through the gap in the hedge, she watched him from her seat on the ground, her lips pursed. His blue eyes, bright and keen, were twinkling with an infectious boyishness. He was a powerfully built man who walked with erect posture, his right hand plunged into the pocket of his light tan suit. The collar of his shirt was unbuttoned, and his tie loosened. Her eyes swept down him all the way to his shining brown shoes.

"I thought you were going out of town today," she commented, closing the book in her lap and clutching it with both hands.

With his left hand he touched his clean-shaven face. "As luck would have it, we settled the case out of court today."

"How convenient," she replied in a dubious tone.

Ignoring her comment, he stepped closer, then said pleasantly, "Mind if I share the fresh air and sunshine with you for a few minutes?" Before she could answer, he settled down beside her, placing his arms behind him and resting the bulk of his weight on them. For a few moments his whole attention seemed focused on the house. Then his head turned slightly toward Barbara. There was a long silence before he fi-

73

nally cleared his throat and said awkwardly, "Uh, you aren't harboring a grudge toward me for last night, are you?"

She considered the question for a moment before answering, "Is there any reason I should?" In spite of herself, she felt a little flush rise to her cheeks.

He stirred. "As I told you already, I didn't mean to embarrass you."

She raised one hand and smoothed the curls at the right side of her head. Then, looking into the inquisitive face beside her, she smiled. "I wasn't too embarrassed. Besides, as I told you, your aunts gave you full credit for the incident. I'd forgotten about it. Really I had."

He laughed, relieved. "My aunts still think of me as a wayward boy in many ways."

"And are you?"

"No." He said the single word without expanding further.

She gazed steadily at him for a moment. At length she spoke, slowly and deliberately. "Why are you so opposed to the book your aunts are proposing?"

"I've told you."

"Then why do I have this feeling there's something more to it than what you've admitted?"

He laughed cheerfully. "I'm supposed to be the attorney? What is this, the third degree?"

"No." She sighed. "But there's more to it than your fear of lawsuits. I'm sure of that."

"Well, if you had a guess, what would you think it would be—that is, if it is something more than possible lawsuits?"

"I haven't the foggiest idea. As far as I can tell, it's truly a harmless project. And to be honest, unless a miracle takes place, it's not going to be something the publishers will do battle over. Believe me, the morning was a disaster."

"So I gathered from the long faces that greeted me inside. However, if I know my aunts, and I do know my aunts, somehow they'll patch everything up by bedtime and be ready to begin again. The family is not one to go to bed with friction among its members. At this moment they are trying to decide how best to bridge the difficulty without either one of them losing too much face."

Barbara smiled. "That's encouraging. I'm not looking forward to the trip back to New Jersey this soon." She shifted her gaze from his face to the ground, but she could feel his eyes holding tightly to her profile. She could have bitten her tongue for saying something so open to suggestive thoughts on his part.

His mouth curved into a slow smile, and his voice was low. "That's good news. Your introduction to our part of the country hasn't been that exciting, has it?"

75

"No," she declared quickly. "But it hasn't been all that bad."

He smiled. "Don't take hope, for I imagine it'll be much worse before it gets better."

She turned to look questioningly at him. "What do you mean by that, John?"

When he looked up at the limbs overhead, Barbara realized he had no intention of answering her inquiry. She said with a tight little smile, "You're quite the man of riddles, aren't you?"

"I know what I know," he half whispered.

"And what is that?" she asked, seeking his eyes with her own.

He still avoided eye contact with her, though she was sure he sensed she was looking at him. Finally he looked down quickly, then away again. "How would you like to go out to dinner with me?" he asked, changing the topic of conversation.

"What?" she demanded, her eyes wide. "And miss one of Lila's delights!"

He chuckled. "When I walked inside a few minutes ago, it smelled like a fish market in there. Tuna?"

"Close." Barbara laughed. "Salmon. I've spent the afternoon trying to keep mine from swimming back upstream."

"Well, it appears to me there will be leftovers for dinner. With that fact in mind you should seriously consider my offer."

"I am seriously considering it." She smiled.

He looked from her face to the limb above their heads again, then back to her face. "I'm wondering," he said with a hint of a smile, "what it is about you that I find so puzzling."

"Oh," she replied, a twinkle in her eyes, "you find me puzzling?"

He stared at her, his expression becoming serious. "The very fact that you're here is puzzling." He inhaled, then asked bluntly, "Why are you here?"

"You know why I'm here," she answered almost inaudibly.

"I know why you say you're here, but why are you really here?" As he stared intently into her eyes, she could see the attorney emerging.

Barbara didn't reply immediately, but when she did, she looked straight into his blue eyes. "Why do I get the feeling you're expecting some kind of confession from me?"

He regarded her for a moment, then said, "I suppose because you're an intelligent, attractive woman, a teacher, a professional, and you've come more than a thousand miles merely to satisfy the whim of two elderly ladies. I just don't accept that explanation. There's more," he ended bluntly.

Avoiding his gaze, she shook her head. "John Michael, I don't know what you expect to hear me say. I've told you the truth. I came because I wanted to come. I'm here because I want to be. There's no mystery, believe me. I needed a quiet time in my life, a time away from home and friends, a time to myself to think."

He nodded and smiled at her and at the same time touched his cheek thoughtfully. "A time to think about what, Barbara?"

She hesitated. She couldn't imagine what he wanted her to say to that question. She had no intentions of divulging her thoughts to him.

"Don't answer that," he said good-naturedly. "I know how women are when they feel as if they're being backed into a corner. In time you'll tell me."

She laughed. "What makes you so sure of yourself?"

His eyes acquired an impish glint as he answered jokingly, "Deductions, my dear, simple deductions." He rose slowly from the ground and, as he stood, brushed off the seat of his pants. "I'll be back for you at seven."

"Oh, you're leaving?"

"I have an errand to run." He smiled down at her. "See you at seven."

She watched him walk down the path, back through the hedge, until the top of his golden head finally disappeared from sight. Somewhat flattered by his interest in her, she was nevertheless determined to begin and end her relationship with John Michael Stewart on a friendly note. The one thing she had most definitely not come a thousand miles in search of was a love affair. She didn't want to be attracted to him or drawn to him in any way.

Minutes after she had heard his car pull out of the drive, she got to her feet and started back toward the house. She noticed Miss Henrietta sitting huddled on the veranda and walked in that direction. Coming closer, she saw the drawn face and eyes fixed in helpless frustration.

When Barbara approached, Henrietta said in tones of dismay, "I see you've been reading."

"Yes." Barbara smiled pleasantly, then held up the book. "Emilie Loring. I found it upstairs in the office."

"Well, I'm happy you've found something to occupy your time, dear. It seems you won't be reading anything from Hannah or me."

Barbara stood back a moment, then stepped up onto the veranda. Speechless, she merely moistened her lips.

The aged gray eyes looked up into hers with an expression of near anguish. "We had so looked forward to accomplishing something in these last years of our lives. And now"—she paused and inhaled deeply, dramatically—"now it's all over. The first day, and it's ended."

"Are you sure?" Barbara said gently as she walked over and seated herself close to the woman.

The gray eyes closed, and Henrietta Stewart sighed deeply. "It would just be the same thing tomorrow and the day after. My sister and I are not seeing eye to eye on this project." Abruptly her lids opened. "That Hannah is a very pig-headed woman, I'll tell you. She wants it to be her way or not at all. I thought we could iron out our differences this afternoon, but she's adamantly opposed to each good idea I have."

Before Barbara could put together a thought, the door to the house swung open, and Hannah rushed out onto the veranda, her cheeks tinted bright pink. "That's just a plain lie, Henrietta Stewart!" she exclaimed hotly. "I may be pig-headed, but you're a plain hog when it comes to this book. You want to tell it all, and what you want me to do is sit quietly and nod my head up and down. Well, I won't do it!"

Barbara parted her lips to speak but slowly closed them when she saw Hannah's hands become firmly planted on her hips.

"You're greedy, Henrietta! You've always been greedy. When we were children, Papa used to—"

"Don't you bring poor dead Papa into this, Hannah! He can't settle any more arguments!"

Barbara's eyes swept from one to the other. Suddenly there was an awful silence, and she could tell from their expressions they were reloading their minds with ammunition to hurl against each other. A bit imploringly she rose in her chair and interrupted with "Ladies, I have an idea."

Both sets of eyes immediately turned to her.

She seized the opportunity and continued quickly in low, soft, nonjudgmental tones. "I realize that it's extremely difficult for any two people to agree exactly in a situation such as this, but one thing is paramount: an agreement on the basis of the project. If you don't mind, I would like each of you to tell me why you undertook this endeavor in the first place."

Henrietta looked first at her sister, who haughtily turned her face out to the afternoon sky.

Barbara cleared her throat and went on. "In order to build anything, one must first lay a proper foundation. In a book it's the theme or the purpose. Otherwise it becomes nothing more than a scattering of words with no direction. Now John Michael told me that the two of you read the book *Peyton Place*, and that your intentions were more or less to expose the life of this community. Is that it?"

Henrietta lifted imploring eyes to her sister, who was still standing. Slowly Hannah's hands left her hips, slid down her sides, and fell limp. A moment passed, and she walked over and sat down on the seat beside her sister. Thoughtfully she rubbed one eye. "I'm afraid that John Michael didn't fully understand what we intended. We did read the book, and we did even make the comment that we could write such a book about our own community. And that's when Henrietta said, 'Oh, Sister, why don't we? It

81

would be so exciting to write a book.' And from that conversation we made up our minds to do this."

"Yes." Henrietta took over the explanation. "But we didn't have in mind to copy the story we had read. I realize that's what John Michael thinks. That was never our purpose. We simply wanted to put what we know about small-town life, and the people of small towns, onto paper. You see, dear, people are very much the same all over. Just as there were elements of greed, infidelity, jealousy, ambition within those characters of that New England town, those same elements are found in a small southern town." She placed her hands limply over her heart. "We know. We've lived our entire lives here. We've seen happy times and sad times, triumphs and tragedies. We've seen it all."

Barbara sat forward on her chair. "See, that's what I'm talking about." Emphatically she went on. "I'm certain in my heart that you two do have something to say, something worthwhile." She paused, searching her mind for the solution to the problem at hand. "And this would be my suggestion to you: that we all work together yet apart on this. For instance, say, in the morning I meet with Miss Henrietta and we work out an outline. Then tomorrow afternoon Miss Hannah and I will take the morning's work and expand it. The next day we'll reverse the situation. That way we could get all the ideas and every two or three days all meet together and go over our progress."

"Oh, my dear!" Hannah exclaimed. "What a marvelous idea." Smiling brightly, she turned to her sister. "Don't you think so, Henrietta?"

"Indeed." Henrietta beamed. "I think it is wonderful. I don't know why we didn't think of it ourselves." After a long sigh of relief she turned to Barbara. "Tell me, dear, where should we begin with our story?"

"At the beginning," Hannah said jokingly, and poked her sister gently in the ribs with her elbow.

"Well, I know that, Sister"—Henrietta laughed pleasantly—"but where is the beginning? In the 1800s or the turn of the century?"

Barbara interrupted thoughtfully. "You know, as bad as it may have seemed, I don't believe this morning was a total loss. There is something about that Wilson woman I found to be intriguing."

Hannah's hand went over her mouth. "Oh, I don't know. I don't think John Michael would want us writing a book about her. Poor thing."

"Why not?" Barbara asked, wide-eyed. "We'll cloak the characters in fiction."

"Of course, we will." Hannah agreed. "And there isn't a better story around than the one about the Wilsons. And you know it as well as I do, Henrietta. The Wilsons could be the pivotal

83

family, and the entire book could turn around them."

Henrietta wrinkled her face into a near grimace. "You know how John Michael is about that family, Hannah. Why, he's always defending those boys on one kind of charge or another. Only last year you remember how he kept that youngest one, Lennie, out of prison on that bootlegging charge."

In exasperation Barbara threw up her hands. "What does your nephew have to do with the story? As an attorney doesn't he defend a number of local people?"

Both women nodded, but it was Henrietta who said, "Yes, but he's a bit touchy about that family for some unknown reason."

Hannah said, "I don't think so, Sister. Our nephew is a good boy. We both know that many of his clients never pay him a cent, so I think it is his nature to look after the less fortunate of the community. I sincerely think we have found the foundation for our story."

After a long pause Henrietta reluctantly agreed. "If you really think so."

"Tell you what," Barbara said brightly, "I've told John that I will go out to dinner with him tonight, and somehow I'll get around to the Wilson family. Perhaps he'll tell me, and then we can reconsider." If by chance there were some unknown legal implications, she wanted to be aware of them from the onset.

An hour later, with the storms of the day calmed, she went upstairs to bathe and dress for the dinner date with John Michael. She was pleased with the way she had managed to smooth over the events of the morning, turning them into excellent prospects for future mornings. She knew she wasn't a great writer, but even as a novice she knew there was a story here. She didn't know how she knew it. She just knew it.

CHAPTER FIVE

Barbara admitted to herself she was beginning to enjoy John Michael Stewart's company. And why shouldn't she? Not only was he pleasing to the eye, but he possessed a certain self-confidence, an inward assuredness about himself that revealed itself outwardly. And she liked his smile.

He drove for a full hour before they arrived at the glass-fronted restaurant overlooking the Tennessee River at the resort area of Pickwick. Although it wasn't even sunset when they left the Stewart house, it was dark when they pulled into the parking lot beside the restaurant. The talk between them had been casual, soft-flowing, on general topics.

The meal that followed was delicious, and the conversation was limited to friendly banter coming from nowhere, leading nowhere. At times Barbara found herself wishing that he were more personal so that she could gain some insight into John Michael.

Then, during coffee and pie, he smiled at her, his eyes radiant in the flickering candlelight. "Are you happy you decided to join me?"

Her "yes" almost bubbled out. "I didn't realize how hungry I was. The dinner was absolutely delicious."

"There's a national park, Shiloh, not far from here. Ever heard of it?"

"One of the Civil War battlesites, isn't it?"

"Yes." He nodded. "I was thinking maybe we could put together a picnic lunch Sunday and come up to spend the day. Would you like that?"

She hesitated and tilted her head slightly. With a smile she said, "I'm not sure Lila will allow me into her kitchen, and I certainly wouldn't want to impose on her to assist with a picnic lunch."

He grinned. "I have a kitchen, and I'll give you a pass into it for such a worthy purpose." He laughed easily. "What's your specialty?"

"Opening cans," she replied laughingly, her blue eyes dancing.

He shook his head. "Then maybe I should take charge of the lunch."

"And I suppose you're some kind of southern Graham Kerr?"

"I'm not embarrassed to say that I can put together a mean bologna sandwich."

She smiled broadly at him. "Sounds as if you

win. I'll leave the main course in your hands, and I'll provide the little extras."

She suddenly felt his gaze change, become more piercing, reaching in and touching something inside her. It was a searching, wondering look. Then he said, "You know every now and then you meet someone that you find attractive at first glance, but the more you see of them, the prettier they become. You have that quality. Did you know that?"

She turned her face away from his stare, separating herself from the peculiar expression he wore. "Thank you," she murmured awkwardly.

"And you're shy too," he added softly.

Looking back at him, she raised her brows slightly, saying, "Not really."

He opened his mouth as if to say something more, then didn't. Instead, his mouth closed, and he looked thoughtful. Thinking now would be an opportune time to bring up a new subject, Barbara inhaled, then plunged into the thought which had been playing at the back of her mind all evening. "You were right about your aunts, John. I believe we've reached an agreeable working arrangement."

She could see a question in his eyes. "And what would that be?"

For the next few moments Barbara explained the working conditions she and the two women had agreed upon earlier in the day. She concluded with "And I think you're mistaken about their purpose in writing this book, John. I don't believe that there is any malice in their hearts toward the community or its people."

"Then what are they attempting to prove?"

"I don't know that they're trying to prove anything. I think, rather, they're attempting to say something about the human nature."

"I daresay they aren't planning to explore the lighter side of humanity."

Barbara spoke honestly. "I don't know. From their conversation this afternoon I'm under the impression that they believe people are pretty much the same everywhere."

John Michael raised his brows sharply. "And that would be rotten, right?"

Pausing, Barbara inhaled. "I don't know what their deepest feelings are, really I don't. I suppose in time I will know, but right now I don't." She hesitated. "I do know, however, that they intend to use one family, fictionalized, of course, for the foundation of their story."

Leaning forward on one elbow resting on the tablecloth, John Michael caught his chin between his thumb and fingers. "Did they say which family?"

"As a matter of fact, they did. A family named Wilson, I believe."

He regarded her for a long moment, then said, "I'm not surprised. I suppose I've known all along that would be their starting point."

"Why do you say that?" Barbara inquired.

He gave a bleak little smile and at the same time shook his head. "Because, my dear little ghostwriter from New Jersey, it is a law of nature that what goes 'round eventually comes 'round."

Her eyes widened. "I'm afraid I don't understand."

"I hope you never understand," he said thoughtfully. "But time will tell, won't it?" Then, quite unexpectedly, he reached over, caught her hand, and squeezed. "Why don't we go walk along the river and stretch our legs a bit before the drive home?"

Barbara pondered his abrupt change in mood as they left the restaurant to walk outside. The path was dark, lined with large river oaks and towering firs, which kept the moonlight from breaking through the dark boughs. "It's a nice night," he commented on a long breath, then reached blindly for her hand and took it in his. He gave one quick, sweeping gaze over her face, then turned his eyes back to the path ahead.

"John Michael," she finally asked, "why are you upset?"

"Did I say I was upset?"

"You don't have to. I don't know you very well, I'll admit, but I do see the change. Besides, the fact that you're breaking my fingers gives me a clue."

He released her hand as if it were a hot coal.

"Sorry," he mumbled. Walking from under the trees on the grassy riverbank, well lighted by the moon, he looked at her face for an instant. Then he stared out at the dark water. "Do you water ski?"

"Not very well," she admitted.

Turning his eyes up to the bright, starry sky, he sighed. "When I was a teenager, a group of us used to spend every weekend up here camping out and skiing." Pointing to the middle of the river, he continued. "That little island was our camping site. We used to row over because we couldn't always afford to rent a boat and motor, but we could always put together enough for a rowboat."

"It's a long way out there," she stated matter-of-factly.

He nodded. "Yes. I remember one time I decided to swim it. I guess I was sixteen or seventeen, young and foolish for sure."

She smiled. "You made it to shore, I see."

He walked a step ahead of her. "Yes, but just barely. About three-quarters of the way my strength gave out. My arms became as heavy as lead, and a thought crossed my mind: *Boy, you're not going to make it.* I'll never forget that moment of panic, sheer panic. My chest felt as if it had been caught in a vise, and I thought for sure my heart would explode wide open. And then, as quickly as I had panicked, a calmness washed over me, and I started again, one stroke

92

at a time. I didn't think about the distance. I merely concentrated on that one stroke, then the next, telling myself, *You can do it, you can do it,* each time I raised my arm out of the water. When I finally made it to shore, I couldn't even pull myself out of the water. I just lay there with my head in the mud, crying and thanking the Lord." He turned his eyes to her and searched her face. "You see, Barbara, few people ever pray to reach the mud, to lay their head in the murk, but sometimes that's what it takes before you can pull yourself up onto the grassy banks."

"What are you saying, John Michael?" she inquired quietly.

"I suppose what I'm saying is that my two wonderful aunts are feeling at the moment that they're drowning in the pool of years. That's why this inner need to do something. Right now I see them reaching for the mud, grabbing in the murk." Suddenly he stopped talking and ducked his head so that his chin almost touched the knot in his tie. "I'm not going to discourage them anymore about this endeavor they have undertaken."

"I—I don't understand," she half whispered.

He turned his head and smiled at her. "I don't expect you to, Barbara, and it isn't something I can explain." He took her hand again, and they walked on along the bank, the breeze from over the water blowing stiffly against their hair. After several hundred feet he said, "I suppose we should start back toward the car." With a short laugh he added, "Five-thirty comes early in the South."

She laughed. "Five-thirty comes early in the North too. I can't believe those two little ladies are such early risers."

"The habit of a lifetime," he commented with a smile.

Standing still beside him, Barbara was comfortable, relaxed, her eyes lingering on the wide river. Suddenly she saw a ring of light flashing in the distance to the right of where they stood, the circle of lights flashing above the dark horizon. "Those look like the lights of a nuclear plant," she said, pointing.

"They are. And a few miles away is the beginning of the Tenn-Tom Waterway. In this day and time even the rivers grow up."

For a moment they stared at each other silently. Then he stepped forward and placed his mouth gently over her lips. Startled at the warmth, she was filled with a sudden disquiet. Immediately she stepped back and looked directly into his eyes. "John, I—" The words died as he reached up to silence her, touching her mouth with his fingertips.

"It was just a kiss, Barbara, not a key. I'm not asking anything from you, not trying to unlock your heart or emotions. I like you and I wanted to kiss you. That's all." His hands dropped to her shoulders, and as he peered into her eyes inquisitively, parts of his face were shadowed in the moonlight.

Without her knowing why, his words were a decided relief to Barbara. How wonderful it was to meet a man who inspired a sense of stability and confidence, yet at the same time a small voice went off in the back of her head, warning her that this was the same man who had brought a woman to the room where she now lived. Growing a bit restive, she said, "I think we probably should head back now, don't you?" Before he answered, she started to walk away from him in the direction of the parking lot.

That night, after she had gone to bed, she thought of him, remembering the soft tone of his voice, studying the intense, handsome lines of his face. John Michael Stewart wasn't like any man she had ever met, and at the same time, try as she might, she couldn't identify the particular quality about him that set him apart from the others.

Late in the afternoon of the next day Barbara sat out on the veranda, going over her notes from the day's dual sessions. Looking up from the pages, she saw a new rose budding in the massive rose garden. A hint of a smile played around the soft lines of her lips. The day had been a complete success, much more productive than she had imagined. Both women had been sweet and cooperative, eager to begin the project in earnest.

Twilight fell, and she sat until the gold and the red of the sunset had faded behind the thick grove of trees to the west. She was just about to rise and go inside when suddenly a movement at the corner of the house caught her eye, and she turned abruptly to see John Michael, dressed in snug-fitting jeans and shiny boots stepping with self-assurance toward her. Her brilliant blue eyes sparkled at him. "What is this?" she said lightly. "The other side of the southern barrister?"

Ducking his head, he answered in an exaggerated drawl, "Why, ma'am, it's good of you to take note that I have another side." Pointing to his chest with all ten fingers, he added mockingly, "This here is the real me."

She laughed softly. "You do a good job of keeping the real you under wraps."

Raising one brow, he grinned crookedly. "Don't we all?" The grin hung on his lips as his gaze slowly moved over her face.

Sensing discomfort, she inhaled the still, rose-scented air in a deep breath. "Are you coming up and sitting down?" she inquired softly.

He silently took the few steps that brought him onto the veranda. When he saw the notebook on her knees, he pursed his lips. "Have a fruitful day?"

"Hmmm, so-so, I guess. We got past a loose outline."

"When will they begin the story, or do you know?" he asked, sitting down beside her.

"The summer of 1914 or actually the spring of that year."

He put one finger thoughtfully to his mouth. "The story of the hundred bales of cotton, right?" He quickly glanced at her, then away.

She smiled. "Right. How did you know?"

He merely shook his head. "Because I know they would do something that stupid." He shrugged. "I knew it." He turned full face to her. "You realize that beginning with a story so well known in this community will eliminate your proposed guise of fiction. Everyone who has lived in this town for more than ten years will know it's the Wilson family."

Her eyes widened. "I can't believe that people will remember some vague story that occurred seventy years ago. For goodness' sake, John, you're too cautious."

"Maybe so," he said impatiently. "But I've discovered it's much better to be cautious in the beginning than sorry in the end." He paused. "However, I didn't come over here to discuss their book. Actually I came to see Lila."

"Lila?"

He nodded. "Yes. I had a letter in the mail that will be of interest to her. Her husband, Rufus, is coming up before the parole board in the next week or so."

"Why, that's wonderful. I'm sure Lila will be delighted with that news, especially in her present elevated mood. I can't believe the change since that trip to the doctor. She was singing at the top of her voice this morning." Then her expression became somewhat doubtful. "Do you think he'll get out?"

"I think his chances are better than fifty-fifty. He's not a bad guy. He merely got caught up in his circumstances and made some bad decisions."

"I suppose that could be said of every inmate, couldn't it?"

His attention became fully focused on her before he swallowed and said, "Could it be that I see the schoolteacher emerging?"

She gave him a testing smile. "And just what are you implying?"

"Nothing," he said with a low chuckle. "I just have this feeling you don't accept excuses when your students show up without their homework."

"I assure you that from the onset of a class," she said crisply, almost in a tone of protest against suspicion, "each student knows from the first day that he or she will be responsible for his or her decisions. I believe in homework as a matter of self-discipline as well as a learning tool. Therefore, if any student shows a lack of this discipline, then the zero he or she receives is a result of his or her choice, not mine."

"A perfectly reasonable and expected explanation," John said easily, a hint of a grin at his lips. "You may be young and pretty, but I have this distinct feeling you're also tough as nails."

Barbara moistened her lips before saying, "For nine months out of the year, John, I deal with the impressionable youth of this country, many of whom are already well shielded by a culture that hides or denies many of the fundamental realities of life."

"Such as?" he asked, stretching out his legs in front and crossing his boots.

Raising one hand, she said emphatically, "Such as exposing the dreamworld many are already enwrapped in by the time they reach my class. They don't know what the real world is, John. They simply don't know. Their attention is drawn to the world's beautiful people, the television stars, the rock singers, the successful scientists who stand before innumerable people and in scientific terms declare the dangers and results of our technology. Their attention is drawn to a false beauty: the dream of making lots of money, wearing the best clothes, driving the most modern, expensive cars, world travel. They come into class with their hair in all shapes and designs and colors, and they slump down in chairs and become bored with Shakespeare and Dickens and Faulkner. And can you or I blame them? They have been totally shielded from reality. They don't know that the world's beautiful people are many times doomed individuals who are in the world's light for a very brief time, that they quickly fade into the darkness of degenerating minds and bodies, that their world is sometimes one of deceit and treachery or hatred and resentment. But who knows this because once they pass through the light, then they are forgotten, and someone new steps into that light? I want my students to become educated not only in English but in life. I want each boy and girl to realize that beyond those few beautiful people, behind that false glamor is a world full of nonbeautiful people, billions of them, people who have no money, people who are hungry, people who don't have cars, people who can't do such a simple thing as take a bath because they have no water. I want them to understand that Shakespeare and Dickens and Faulkner were not just writers but true artists who were blessed with a talent to paint a real picture of the human condition. And it's real, as real today as it was then. Technology changes and advances. Everything progresses but the human condition."

When she stopped speaking, he regarded her so fixedly, so silently that she began to wonder if she had said something which offended him. He hesitated in his silence for a while longer, then asked softly, "Barbara, I wouldn't want you to think I'm badgering you with this question, but tell me, why are you here?"

She responded first with a quick, fading smile. Finally she said, "I came to help your aunts write a book."

"Why don't I believe you?"

"You don't believe that I'm here as a ghost-writer?"

He smiled. "Oh, yes, I believe that, but I know that there is more, some other reason that you aren't telling me about. It doesn't make sense that someone who has it all together as you do would be spending a summer doing what you're doing." His brows rose inquisitively, and his eyes softened. "Don't you trust me?"

Barbara looked over at him as if uncertain what to say.

He went on, smiling. "Perhaps it's my conditioning, but I know when someone is evading the real issue. You're here in my state this summer for a particular reason that has nothing to do with your summer job. Your job merely made it convenient for you to be here."

She smiled back at him. "Am I being cross-examined?"

"No." He chuckled, drawing his legs back up, then starting to get up from the chair. "I would never cross-examine such a pretty lady outside the courtroom. However, I might offer to be her friend." As he began to step from the veranda, he looked back at her and said, "My granddad

101

used to say, 'A good friend is better to have around than a gallon of home brew.'"

"I'll remember that if I'm tempted to drink home brew," she said laughingly.

He waved one hand at her, heading toward the back of the house. "Well, I'm off to see Lila. Maybe I can make her day."

After his head had disappeared behind a tall shrub, Barbara glanced down at the notebook on her lap, then raised her eyes back to the roses. With an unconscious gesture she covered her mouth with the fingers of her right hand. Who was John Michael Stewart? Had she come a thousand miles to allow him into her life? Was she afraid of his offer of friendship? What was his definition of a friend? So many questions. Above all, Barbara considered herself a realist. She had no doubt she was becoming more and more attracted to him, more and more aware of the drawing qualities of his personality. She could feel the quickening of her pulse in his presence, the growing disquiet of her mind and thoughts. But she was still in full control of her situation, and she intended to remain at the helm of her own emotions. She had been through some of love's disillusions. She had experienced the power of passion which overcame rational thought. She had given way to desire only to search later for love in the relationship and find it missing, discovering it had never been there. She wanted more than that because she was more than that. It had taken the biggest part of her life to uncover the real Barbara Whitney, but now that she had found her, she was unwilling to compromise her. She wanted love in her life. Love, the real thing, not some imitation. In her deepest being she knew love was a beautiful, shining diamond, and she was no longer willing to settle for a rhinestone. Her growing attraction to John Michael Stewart would require care and caution on her part. The best remedy for temptation was to avoid it from the onset.

That evening she sat at the dinner table with her two employers, looking down at the feast Lila had whipped up after learning of the news of the parole hearing from John Michael. Although the two women had tried to coax their nephew into staying for the meal, he had excused himself with a grin and a quick wink toward Barbara, who had just entered the hallway. She mouthed "Chicken" silently at him, then watched as he left the house, chuckling under his breath.

After dinner Barbara accompanied the two women into the living room for a quick "chat," as Henrietta put it. Both the Stewarts were a bit excited about the day's accomplishments as well as the news of Lila's husband's possible release. Barbara seated herself comfortably in a chair, then watched as the two flitted about like little hummingbirds before finally settling down beside each other on the couch.

"This has been a good day." Hannah smiled happily. "I feel so much has been accomplished."

Henrietta agreed chirpily. "Indeed. This is exactly as I imagined it would be. Our work has begun, and now this good news about Rufus."

Barbara nodded, smiling agreeably.

Suddenly serious, Henrietta looked at her. "You won't be uncomfortable with an ex-con running about, will you, dear?" she asked bluntly.

After only the slightest hesitation Barbara answered, "I wouldn't think so."

"Well, rest assured he's not a hardened man in the criminal sense. He's just hardheaded. Lila warned him that if he kept writing those bad checks, sooner or later he would give one to someone who would expect him to make it good. And that's exactly what happened when he went over to Corinth and wrote a bad check for a color television set for Lila's birthday."

Hannah took up the story at that point. "Of course, Lila's gift was much more than he imagined: a long rest from him." Shaking her head, she concluded. "And the poor thing had to give back the television set. I told John Michael that it seemed that if a man had to go to prison for giving his wife a present, the wife should at least get to keep the present. Of course, John Michael didn't agree, so the television had to go." Turning to her sister, she said, "When we decide on a salary for Rufus, why don't we make sure we pay him enough to buy that television?"

"We could do that." Henrietta agreed happily. "Maybe start him off with a bonus of sorts. After all, he will be getting out for good behavior."

Hannah hesitated before saying with a little less enthusiasm, "Maybe we should ask John Michael about it before we decide positively. After all, he is Rufus's attorney."

Henrietta nodded agreeably, still smiling. "We'll do that. He said he would see us in the morning. We'll ask him then."

"He never comes over on Sunday mornings, Sister. Are you sure you heard him correctly?"

Clearing her throat, Barbara interjected, "He's coming over to get me." When both sets of eyes turned to her, she felt obliged to offer an explanation. "He's taking me to the Shiloh battlesite for a picnic."

Both women looked at each other, then back at Barbara.

Feeling a bit awkward under their gazes, Barbara shifted and asked softly, "Does that surprise you?" They were certainly looking at her strangely.

"No, dear, it doesn't surprise us, but the last young woman our nephew took on a picnic at that park—" Stopping abruptly, Hannah let the word *park* dangle in midair.

"Oh, dear." Henrietta sighed. "You might as

105

well go ahead and tell her so she might know what to expect at that place."

Barbara sat forward in her chair, her eyes narrowing, waiting.

"Well," Hannah said stoutly, "the last young woman he took on a picnic ended up living in this house, and most of the time with him. Not that Henrietta or I agreed with it, but after all, he is our nephew, and he didn't want to take her to his farm because of his image."

"So he brought her here," Hannah stated angrily, "and ruined all our images. Sister and I had to tell the most outrageous lies to protect the Stewart name, then more lies to cover the one we started out with. I never was so relieved in my life as I was the day that young woman came to her senses and ran off."

"Well," Barbara said firmly, "I assure you both that regardless of the charm he displays at a picnic, he will not be sharing my room."

"Whew." Henrietta sighed. "I do so hate to tell lies, especially in church."

"Such a relief," Hannah said, sighing just as her sister had. "Besides, I've never seen anything romantic at one of those dreadful sites. After all, it's only a place where a bunch of men fought and died and many are buried. But John Michael has always loved that battleground from the time he was a young boy."

"I don't think it's because of the graves, Sister. I think it's because of the scenery, especially the river. He spent a lot of time there, swimming, fishing, and doing all those things young boys love to do."

Later that night after typing the outline, Barbara entered the bedroom. The expression on her face tightened as her eyes crept moodily over the furniture, coming to a halt on the bedspread. She probably could have gained any amount of information she'd desired about John Michael tonight downstairs, but for some reason she could not make herself ask a single question. That was very strange for her because her nature was one of inquisitiveness.

CHAPTER SIX

In late morning, with the bright sun hovering almost directly overhead, Barbara sat on the grassy riverbank a foot or so from John Michael, who was silently staring out at the deep blue water. Together, slowly and deliberately, they had spent the past two hours walking along the paths of the large battleground, now a national park with towering old trees and quiet, restful trails weaving in and out among the trees all the way down to the riverside.

After a few moments he turned to her, his blue eyes radiantly soft in the sunlight. "It's hard to believe a place so peaceful, with such serene beauty, could have ever been obscured with the gray smoke of muskets and cannons, that the pond back there could have actually turned red from human blood flowing into it. But it's a fact it happened. The water actually turned red."

When he paused, she said in a low voice, "I

find all old battlefields to be that way, John, at least all the ones I've visited. It's almost as if the land itself came to mock the events which took place on them. Look how quiet and peaceful it is now."

He pulled up a single blade of grass and began to strip it from its center vein outward. One side of his mouth rose in a little smile. Then he said, "When I was a youngster, I would get so mad at the goverment for burying all our Confederate soldiers in those large community graves while they laid all the Union troops in those neat marked single ones near that chapel. And then one trip I went inside the Union cemetery and saw that grave of the little drummer boy who was killed during the battle, and I thought the world must have been crazy if parents would have allowed their little child to go to war, to beat a drum while men killed each other, and then to be killed himself. I couldn't make any sense of it."

She met his gaze solemnly. "And can you now?"

He smiled and shook his head slowly from side to side. "No, but at present I've quit trying to. The past is best forgotten except as a history lesson."

She laughed softly. "So that we can learn from our mistakes."

His smile widened. "I wish."

She tilted her head slightly toward her right

shoulder. "Are we still talking about the war, John?" Then she flushed, realizing she had taken the initiative to change the conversation from general to personal.

For a moment he sat looking at her in silence, then said thoughtfully, "And would you like to know about me, Barbara?"

She nervously moistened her lips with her tongue. Giving a tiny shrug, she answered, "Only if you'd like to tell me about yourself."

He chuckled and stretched his long legs out in front of him. "I thought you'd never ask." He looked at her jokingly, his lips twisted in a grin, then relaxed before he said, "And where would you like me to begin?"

After another tiny shrug she said, "Just jump in anywhere you feel comfortable." She smiled at him.

Folding his hands together, he said, "I'm thirty-four years old. I've never been married except," he said sheepishly, "in the minds of my dear old aunts, who told everyone at one point that I was and then, when we parted ways, made up all kinds of tales of how she left me because of a wild streak she had and that she had gotten a quick divorce in Reno. And I don't know what all they did tell. But actually we were never married."

"Did she run off?" Barbara asked when he paused for breath.

He laughed out loud. "You already know about her, don't you?"

"She's been mentioned." Barbara smiled, looking at his face calmly.

He continued to laugh. "Those two! What am I going to do with them? What did they tell you?"

"Oh, just bits and pieces, here and there." Barbara found herself also laughing.

Inhaling deeply, he shook his head. "The truth is that she and I did plan to be married, but then we discovered a great obstacle in our relationship."

"And what was that?" Barbara pressed the issue, feeling she was intruding, wanting to and not wanting to at the same time.

"We discovered we didn't love each other, not the kind of love a marriage requires. We liked each other tremendously, and we had a good time together, but it was a very superficial relationship. The first crisis we faced together was the end for us. It was really that simple."

"I see," Barbara said simply, somehow sensing that she actually did. How well she herself knew the feeling.

He turned his gaze back to the river. "You know, Barbara, I was reared in a small southern town, grew up, went to high school, but by the time I went off to college I had already begun to allow my life to be influenced by negative truths. Listening to you yesterday on the veranda talking about your students today reminded me of myself sixteen years ago. I had already turned my eyes away from the basic truths of life, the positive truths by the time I reached eighteen."

"Why, John?" she asked in little more than a whisper.

"I don't know." He lapsed into silence for a moment, then went on. "I had no real reason to doubt the truths I had been reared by. My dad was a dairy farmer, and a very successful one, a God-fearing man, strong, yet tenderhearted. My mother died the summer I was graduated from high school, and I think watching her during her illness that year before her death restructured my whole pattern of thinking."

"Are you an only child, John?"

He nodded and sighed. "Yes, but I don't believe that was a significant factor in my life. I was never lonely for friends. As a matter of fact, I was never lonely. I didn't know what the emotion was until I entered college, away from home and friends."

"Where did you go to school?" she asked easily, leaning her weight back on her arms.

"Southern Miss and then Emory in Atlanta. After the bar exam I worked in the capital for a large corporate firm. You know"—he paused, and his eyes searched heavenward—"I had decided money was the answer to everything, so I made up my mind to become a millionaire by my twenty-ninth birthday. I had quite a large sum of money left to me by my grandfather, who incidentally was my aunts' oldest brother, so I took the money and made some investments in the stock market and bought some land here and there for speculative purposes. To be honest, I was a millionaire by the time I was twenty-seven. I was on top of the world." He gestured loosely with one hand out toward the water, adding, "Or so I thought."

Barbara was unable to hide her surprise, and her lips parted slightly as she looked thoughtfully at him. He looked the part of a millionaire less than anyone she had ever seen.

He talked on. "And for the next three years I lived the life of a true-blue playboy. I bought things, and I used people. I had a penthouse. I traveled all over the world. I dressed in the latest fashions, drove the best cars." Suddenly his eyes swung around to look at her, and he smiled sadly. "But you know what, Barbara, it seemed the more I gained, the more I traveled, the more things I bought, the more people I used for my own pleasure, the emptier I became. Deep within, a void was forming, a bottomless, growing emptiness. I was the loneliest man alive, isolated by my own negative truths."

"What changed you, John?" she asked as he lapsed into momentary silence.

"Four years ago I was in Japan on a high-flying business trip." The words slowed and emerged painfully. "I remember I was lying in my bed, staring up at the ceiling, wondering what was wrong with the world. You see, I knew something had to be wrong with the world for me to feel so rotten when I had so much. It couldn't be that anything was wrong with me, so it had to be the fault of the world. And then my phone rang, and it was Aunt Henrietta telling me my dad had suffered a heart attack and was in extremely critical condition. I can't explain how I felt. It was as if all the weight of the world had collapsed on me. I was half the world away, and my dad was dying. In that moment nothing meant anything to me except getting home. For hours and hours I was in the air or trying to make connections at each airport. It took me thirty hours from the time of the call to arrive at the hospital in Memphis where they had taken my dad. I got in to see him just before he died, and his only words to me were 'Son, take care of your aunts. They'll soon be all alone in this world, and that shouldn't happen to anybody.'"

Barbara gazed at him solemnly. "And that's what you did?" she inquired softly.

Surprisingly he gave a few quick shakes of his head. "Not right away," he answered in a whisper. "You see, Barbara, it was a frustrating request. It was as if my dad had asked me to give up everything I had worked for, my career and all the trimmings, to come back to this small town and look after two old ladies. I thought it was an unfair request, even from a dying man. So after a few days of inner struggle I dropped by their house and told them I had to get back to Washington and that I would call them often, and I told them how they could get in touch with me if anything came up. I knew they wouldn't bother me, so it was just a gesture I made, more or less in an attempt to soothe my conscience." Suddenly he rose to his feet and, brushing off the seat of his jeans, walked down the bank to the edge of the water. He looked first at the water, then back at her. "But when I got back to the capital, I soon realized that money had become secondary. It had slipped a notch or two on my list of priorities. After burying my dad, I became interested in finding out the truth behind life, all the typical questions anyone asks when faced with death. When my mother died, I had been a kid, but my dad died when I was thirty, or near my birthday at any rate, so the impact was much greater emotionally. I wanted to know my real purpose in life, the truth behind all the rumors floating around the world as to the reason for life."

Spellbound, Barbara continued to stare at him.

Suddenly he grinned at her. "Now I know this must be boring, so why don't we spread lunch and eat? I have the summer to fill you in on what happened next in the life and times of John Michael Stewart."

116

She laughed quietly.

"You have a beautiful laugh." The words came softly from his mouth.

She lifted her eyes to meet his, and an overwhelming silence followed as they stared at each other. Then he approached her and slowly lowered himself to his knees beside her. She was speechless, holding fast to his eyes, trying to fight the deep trembling coming to life, upsetting her innermost emotions.

He reached out and touched her cheek with the back of his fingers and leaned forward. "Wouldn't it be a shame not to kiss a mouth as pretty as yours on a day as perfect as this?" he whispered.

Her expression became troubled, unsure. She bent her head a little to avoid his probing gaze. He caught both her hands in his, then bent forward and pressed his lips into the softness of her dark hair. She felt his breath warm the top of her head, and that warmth reached to the bottom of her toes. Gripped with a strange uneasiness, she brought her face up slowly, her blue eyes darting searchingly to his. "John," she began softly, "I don't know that this is wise."

"I never professed to be a wise man," he said teasingly. "However, I know one thing: I won't be going after the picnic basket, not until you kiss me."

"That's blackmail," she whispered.

"I know." He smiled. "A little something I

picked up from one of my clients. My lips are the way to the food basket."

Her hands drew away from his, and she put them at the sides of his face. There was no denying that she was going to kiss him. She knew beyond a shadow of any doubt she was, and she also knew that this kiss would be different from the others because the foundations of her emotions were changing. His gaze was melting her heart, and unhurriedly she placed her mouth very close to his, so close that breaths mingled as she said, "I'm going to do this only one time, John."

Smiling, he whispered hoarsely, "Then you should know I'm very much like a Lay's potato chip: No woman can kiss me just once."

"We'll see." She accepted his jesting challenge as her lips touched his with the lightness of the fragrant air around them, pressing softly and slowly as her fingers tightened on his face. That kiss hushed the world about them. She had merely touched his mouth, but in the next second his lips fiercely smothered hers. She became completely absorbed with his mouth, with his lips crushing hers, first roughly, then with a sweeping gentleness. There was nothing familiar about the feeling grasping her, the warmth dancing through her body.

His arms went around her tightly, and her hands slid from his face to his neck as mouths continued to strain anxiously against each other with an electric spark that promised to ignite. Then, with a sudden quickness, he pulled away from her. "Barbara . . . I—I—"

"What is it?" she asked, gazing at him with some bewilderment. The tremor had moved from her body to her voice. "Is something wrong?"

He didn't answer. Instead, he stared at her with almost the same measure of bewilderment in his eyes as that which she knew was in hers. And then he rose slowly to his feet, his eyes not leaving hers. "I'll go get lunch," he said, giving his head a quick shake as if he were clearing away cobwebs.

She blinked and said with a calmness she didn't feel, "Good." She watched as he moved away from her, his hands sliding into his back pockets.

When he was gone from sight, she turned her darkening eyes to the river. He had pulled away from her. He had been the one to end the kiss. A near frown settled on her face. Why had he coaxed her into the kiss and then responded the way he had? It certainly wasn't a very flattering thing to happen. Yet she knew that the kiss had affected him as deeply as it had her. Waiting for him to return, she was puzzled and found herself feeling almost desolate.

They had left the park by midafternoon and started for home. After the morning of their sharing a special closeness, the afternoon had

119

seemed strained, only splattered with insignificant conversation. He had pulled far away from her, and she simply didn't understand why.

When they arrived at his aunts' home, John Michael walked her as far as the front door, then gave her a quick peck on the cheek before saying, "Thank you for a most enjoyable day."

"Aren't you coming inside?" she asked, surprised to see him turn.

He gave a brief shake of his head. "No, I'm going to get on back home." At the top step he turned and looked at her but said nothing. Then he turned again and walked swiftly to his car.

She stood, feeling absolutely helpless, watching him leave. As she moved inside the doorway, she heard a voice call out from the living room, "Barbara, is that you, dear?"

Swallowing hard, she forced herself to smile. "Yes," she answered.

"Well, good." Henrietta reached the door by the time her words did. Peering out with a bright expression, she said, "I was hoping you would come home early. I feel creative. Do you think we might work awhile on the book before Sister and I leave for church?"

Barbara nodded, her smile becoming bleaker.

Late in the night Barbara sat at her typewriter, looking over the pages of notes she'd taken during the impromptu session with Henrietta. She had some difficulty with her concentration because her mind kept returning to the morning and the time spent with John Michael. He had been in such a wonderful, talkative mood, up until the time of the kiss. Then the change in him had been radical. Why? She knew she hadn't done anything to offend him. He had been the one to pursue the touch in the first place. Feeling a tinge of irritation, she turned again to the notes and began reading over the tale of the hundred bales of cotton. After a few paragraphs she leaned back in her chair and turned her eyes to the ceiling. *What makes us so stupid?* She sighed. Before her eyes was the story of one man's stubbornness, which had brought utter destruction to his family. However, by the time she concluded her night's work she had sensed an emotional leveling of the inner turmoil she felt about John Michael.

After she had gone to bed, she lay awake for a long time thinking not about John Michael but rather about the man with the hundred bales of cotton. Andrew Wilson. As Henrietta Stewart related the story, Andrew had been a big, stubborn man who had put his all into regaining a part of the Wilson land which had been lost during the Reconstruction Era in the South. After borrowing heavily to purchase a portion of the land, a hundred acres, to be cultivated, he planted the entire acreage in cotton. A man with a wife and five children, he obviously accepted his responsibility as head of the family.

Three of his children were boys, all teenagers, and with their help in the fields, when fall came, a hundred bales of cotton were harvested and taken to the gin for processing. But the local banker, who had made the loan to Andrew, had also passed on the information that cotton was going to sell for a dollar a pound within the year. After mulling over the information from the banker, Andrew and his sons brought the cotton back home and stored the bales in the barn instead of taking it to market. The wait for the price to climb began. Andrew had calculated that when he sold his cotton for a dollar a pound, he would have enough money not only to live comfortably for years ahead but also to be able to buy back the remainder of the Wilson land.

Barbara fell asleep thinking of all the bales of cotton stacked neatly in the large, weather-beaten Wilson barn. The next morning she was back at her typewriter bright and early before breakfast, in an attempt not to fall behind on her part of the bargain.

Lucky for her, she got some work in before breakfast because at the table the roof fell in again on the two sisters. Barbara unknowingly initiated the rift when Hannah said to her as she entered the dining room, "My dear, you look bright and chipper this morning."

Smiling, Barbara answered, "I've been up for a couple of hours working on the notes from yesterday."

Hannah turned stiffly to her sister. "What notes from yesterday? Don't tell me you work on Sunday."

Henrietta, buttering a biscuit, said sweetly, "While you were napping, Sister, Barbara and I worked on the first chapter after she came home from her picnic with John Michael."

Hannah's face fell even more. "I can't believe that you would do this behind my back, while I was sleeping no less. Henrietta, it's just in your blood to be a sneak."

Barbara tried to bridge the growing rift. "It's not finished, Miss Hannah. Really. We just worked on the background more or less. Uh, I intended to type the notes and go over them with you in the morning."

Hannah's mouth drew into a pouting line. Finally she said, "I suppose she told you about the cotton, how Andrew and his boys stored it in the barn and waited for the price to go up."

Toying with the egg on her plate, Barbara nodded reluctantly.

Henrietta sat across the table, eating like a frisky filly, while Hannah sat back, squaring her shoulders, and said, "And I suppose she told you how the price did begin to rise that year and how when it did, his poor wife begged him to sell."

Even more reluctantly Barbara nodded.

"Well, that does it!" Hannah exclaimed. "I wash my hands of this entire thing. If Henrietta is going to be the hog, she can most certainly have all the slop."

"Hannah." Henrietta turned calmly to her sister, "Papa used to tell you that you would sleep your life away. You've been slothful and lazy all your life. Now don't blame this sweet young lady, or me, because we refuse to wallow in a bed when there are things to be done. I didn't tell the whole story. I told it only halfway, leaving the last part for you to tell—that is, if you can keep yourself awake long enough to tell it."

At that point Lila's head emerged through an opening in the door, and she called out, "Y'-all need anything in here?"

"You might bring me a cup of coffee." A deep voice boomed from behind Barbara's chair. She turned slowly to look into the smiling face of John Michael. "Morning," he said directly to her, then walked over and pulled out the chair beside her.

"I'm glad you're here, John Michael," Hannah said, eyeing her sister coolly. "I want you to draw up a contract."

After thanking Lila for the cup of very black coffee she placed in front of him, he raised his eyes to his aunt. "What kind of contract?" he asked pleasantly.

"To protect my interest from a pure hog."

"Your interest in what, Aunt Hannah?" he asked innocently.

"My interest in this book Henrietta is trying to write without me."

"And while you're drawing up that contract," Henrietta said primly, "you might insert a clause to protect my interest from a particular female Rip Van Winkle I know."

"What's going on here?" he asked, looking first at one, then at the other. Finally his eyes came to rest on Barbara, who merely shrugged innocently.

After receiving simultaneous explanations from his two aunts, he shook his head, saying firmly, "Hold it, just hold it."

Both women lapsed into silence.

Inhaling a deep breath, he said, "Aunt Henrietta, Aunt Hannah, do you realize that in the past few days you've argued more and been mad at each other more than I can ever recall in my entire thirty-four years. Why do you suppose that is?"

Henrietta answered quickly. "Because sometimes it takes eighty-two years really to get to know someone, and that's exactly how long it's taken me to get to know Hannah Stewart."

"That's impossible," Hannah interrupted. "Since I'm only eighty, it couldn't have taken you more than eighty years, and that explains what the situation is, John Michael. Most of the time she doesn't know what she's saying."

"Well, from all I can see and hear," John said

forcefully, "I think you both should reconsider this endeavor and its effects."

Almost in an instant the two women became allies. "It isn't this endeavor," Hannah said much more quietly. "Not at all."

"Indeed not." Henrietta agreed readily. "It's just that I suppose we've become caught up in the creative aspects, and it's possible we're becoming temperamental in our later years."

"I'm sure that's it," Hannah added. "I hear all artists are temperamental. I don't think you should expect your aunt and me to be different, John Michael. And now that I think about it, I don't think your idea about the contract is a good idea at all."

His eyes widened.

"Nor do I." Henrietta joined in. "So forget the contract. I'm sure you can find plenty to do today without that."

He gave his head a couple of tiny shakes, then picked up his cup of coffee and took a slow swallow. "I came here this morning to see if you two could spare Barbara."

"Spare her for what?" Hannah inquired, peering closely at her nephew.

"I'm going down to the state prison to talk with Rufus, to prepare him for the parole board meeting later this week. I thought she might like to come along, give her a chance to see a little-traveled part of the state."

"Dear, you don't want to go to prison, do you?" Henrietta asked point-blank.

Looking down at her plate, Barbara considered for a moment. "Actually I wouldn't mind seeing a prison from the inside," she answered truthfully.

After a long silence Hannah sighed. "Oh, dear." She pursed her lips, then relaxed. "John Michael, we're going to let her go with you this one time, but from now on you must remember that Miss Whitney is our employee, and we need her here if we're going to get on with our book."

"That's right." Henrietta agreed. "So you take her to prison with you today, but after today, it's hands off, young man."

He chuckled. "Okay. You've got yourself a deal."

Hannah leaned forward. "You won't take Lila, too, will you? I mean, after all, we do need someone here with us."

His brows rose. "No, I hadn't planned on taking Lila. I want Rufus to keep his mind on what I'm telling him. I'm afraid Lila might divert his attention." His voice dropped to a whisper. "As a matter of fact, maybe we should keep this visit our little secret. After all, there's no guarantee Rufus will be granted his parole. No need to build Lila's hopes up needlessly."

"We won't breathe a word," Hannah whispered back.

Henrietta nodded agreeably. "Goodness, no."

Barbara got up from her chair. "Well, if you'll excuse me, I'll go upstairs and change."

"No need for that," John Michael said with a smile. "You look fine. Down here in this part of the country we rarely dress up when we go to prison."

Barbara hesitated at the doorway. "Still, if you don't mind, I would prefer to change—that is, if you have time."

"I have all the time in the world," he said pleasantly. "Go ahead. I want you to be comfortable. And while you're upstairs, you might pack an overnight bag in the event Rufus goes before the board tomorrow."

"In that event she can't go, John Michael Stewart," Henrietta said firmly and quickly.

Barbara hung in the doorway, stunned by his remark. She raised her eyes to follow the conversation taking place at the table.

"Indeed, she can't," Henrietta said equally firmly. "I won't hear of it. This young lady is here in our care, and none of your hanky-panky will be tolerated."

"And Sister is perfectly correct," Henrietta said.

"You mean you'd rather have me drive all the way to the prison today and, if Rufus's hearing is scheduled tomorrow, drive back in the morning, knowing it's a four-hour drive?" John Michael put forth his argument with a faint gesture

128

of his hand in the air. "For goodness' sake, I'm your nephew. You can trust me."

"Young man, we know your track record. If you aren't planning on bringing her back tonight, then we won't allow her to go. Understand?"

"Okay . . . okay. I know when I'm done for. We'll be back tonight." He chuckled. "But it's time for you two to forget—and forgive."

With a smile on her lips Barbara started up the stairs to change her clothes.

CHAPTER SEVEN

The trip to the state prison was an absolute delight for Barbara. John Michael was in such a happy mood, telling one funny story after another. He kept her laughing almost constantly during the first hour of the trip. Then, suddenly, out of the blue, she looked at him, at his profile, and the laughter faded momentarily. Her lips parted with solemnity as a strange little sensation tugged at her heart. In that instant it occurred to her that her feelings for John Michael Stewart were beginning to run much deeper than she cared to admit, even to herself. It occurred to her that what she was beginning to feel for him was a new feeling, one she had not experienced before. A question just kind of slipped across her mind: *Am I falling in love with him?* Then, without waiting for the answer, she tore her eyes away from him and looked out her side window until her mind once again became absorbed in the present moment.

By midmorning they had left the Mississippi hill country behind and entered the delta. As they drove along the straight, flat highway, she gazed out at the smooth, rich land which stretched from horizon to horizon. "My goodness, there isn't a hill or even a rise anywhere," she commented softly.

He smiled at her, a broad, open smile, full of enjoyment. "You should see it in the fall just before harvest. It looks like a giant patchwork quilt with its white cotton and green corn and sunburned soybeans. At one time it was all white. I can remember when I was a boy, my dad had friends in the delta we would visit, and I loved looking at the cotton in full bloom." He inhaled deeply. "But now the crops have become so diversified it isn't that way anymore. Yet it's still pretty in the fall," he said.

She raised a hand to brush back a fallen strand of hair near her eyes, and her fingers lingered at the side of her face. They were silent for the next few miles, and John Michael kept giving her quick glances, his eyes narrowing thoughtfully at her. Several miles down the two-lane highway, he said, "Barbara, you do realize I'm becoming very fond of you, don't you?"

Making no reply, she turned and looked at him uneasily, apprehension tightening her expression. She had to work at it before she could muster a faint smile. Fond? That was such an unusual word to use in a relationship between a man and a woman. In fact, it was the first time any man had ever spoken that particular word to her, and she wasn't exactly sure of his meaning, what he was trying to imply.

He stared at her profile, a questioning glint coming to life in his blue eyes. "I didn't steal you away from my aunts this morning to prevent work on their book. I wanted you to be with me."

Growing more uncomfortable with the serious drift of the conversation, she inhaled deeply before saying, "I think we'll have adequate time in the weeks ahead to finish the book."

"Barbara," he said explosively, catching her completely off guard, "why are you such a private person? Aren't you ever going to talk to me about *you*?"

"I don't know what you mean, John," she answered quickly.

"It's really very simple. Do you realize that you carefully guard each word you speak, that the person speaking the words remains cloaked, hidden? Like the other day, for instance, you gave me an insight into your teaching philosophy, and your single-mindedness about my aunts and their so-called project has given me some glimpse of your determinedness, but it's as if the real you were continually wrapped in some kind of mystery."

"I'm not a mystery, John," she said in little more than a whisper.

"Then tell me why you're here."

She gave him a small smile. "You are persistent, aren't you?"

"Have you ever met an attorney who wasn't?"

A short pause ensued. "What do you expect me to say in answer to that question?"

He shrugged. "I don't know." Then his brows lifted, and he smiled. "The truth."

Sighing, she said, "The truth is, there is no great mystery about why I came South this summer. I simply needed to get away from familiar surroundings."

"Why?"

"Because this year was a very hard year for me."

"In what way?"

"In many ways. I had difficult classes. I've had emotional crises that I've not faced before. So many things came at me this year that I finally wanted to remove myself from familiar surroundings and come somewhere new in order to clear my head, to think out some things that have been bothering me for a while."

"What kind of things?" He kept pressing on.

"John Michael, I'm one of several children. My entire family is large: aunts, uncles, cousins, nieces, nephews. A real family gathering at my home sometimes consists of forty or fifty people. Because I am one of the few members of my family who are still single, I get bombarded at each gathering with questions such as 'Why, Barbara, is there any special young man this year?'; 'Barbara, dear, have you given up on marriage?' Or, 'Barbara, your uncle and I were hoping to see you with a wedding band on before your thirtieth birthday.' And then two or three times each year I visit a hospital and look through a glass at the newest member of the family. I don't know how to explain it without sounding absolutely silly, but I was beginning to question the priorities of my life. But as long as I was home, so to speak, pushed and pulled in different directions, I became more confused by my own thoughts. Then one night I was in my apartment alone, grading tests, to be exact, when I just dropped my pen and pushed myself back from the desk and asked aloud, 'What am I doing here?' And that question was followed by the classic one."

He smiled and interjected softly, "Why was I born?"

She nodded vigorously several times. "Yes, exactly. In that instant life made no sense at all to me. I became suspended in a moment that made me weak all over."

"What did you do?"

"The easiest thing I could. I blamed my current state of mind on stress, and I got up from the desk, went into my kitchen, and poured a cup of coffee. I sat down at the table and picked up a magazine I had purchased from the super-market, but you know, John, something very strange happened when I lifted it."

His eyes widened. "What?"

"Well, when I buy magazines, I usually pick up two copies, one of which I give to my next-door neighbor, an elderly woman on a fixed in-come with a special love for women's magazines with the recipes and all that. I had bought a popular women's magazine, thinking I had pur-chased two, but when I lifted my copy, there was a different magazine under it. A magazine for writers. Now isn't that strange?"

He laughed. "Not any stranger than what hap-pened to me in Calcutta, India, four years ago."

Startled, she stared at him. "India? You've been to India?"

He nodded slowly, a faraway smile on his lips. "Four years ago, Barbara, India separated me from my millionaire status. You know I told you that after my dad's death I went back to Wash-ington to my work at the firm. Well, it just so happened that in my absence a new junior part-ner was brought in, and almost immediately we struck up a friendship. Outwardly he was the most all-together guy I had ever met. His name was Frank Perry. I didn't know what he had, but I knew I was envious of whatever it was. Noth-ing shook the guy. I remember one day we were in the office library, and he was sitting there, staring into space with a blank expression on his face, as if he had escaped into some other realm, some other dimension of life. Then, after a few moments, he gave his head a little shake and became attentive to the research. I just came right out and asked him what he was doing. He seemed happy to tell me. He was meditating. He went on to tell me how he had found true peace." Suddenly his hands gripped the steering wheel fiercely, then relaxed. Turning to her, he smiled. "Ah, but that's a long story, and I'd rather hear the sound of your voice. You were saying the second magazine was a writer's magazine."

She sighed softly. "Yes. I remember thinking: *How in the world did I end up with this thing?* I don't know what made me pick it up and start thumbing through it, but I found it rather interesting. I read a couple of the articles, and from there I started reading the ads. That's where I discovered the one your aunts sent in for a ghostwriter. At first I gave it not even a passing thought because even though I've always had some writing aspirations, I've been perfectly content to be a teacher. But after I went to bed that night, for some reason the ad popped back into my mind, and it was as if some little voice inside me said, 'Barbara, you could do this.' " She shrugged. "And you know the story from there. A week or so later I contacted your aunts, and here I am."

He laughed. "On your way to prison."

She also laughed. "Are you trying to tell me something?"

He gave a mocking shake of his head. "Not me. I like having you here so much that the book is beginning to slip farther and farther from my mind."

Still laughing, she said, "I have severe reservations about its completion. Thus far we have only gotten past the burning of the cotton."

A somewhat somber expression slid down over his face. "Wasn't that something?"

She turned to him, the curve of laughter also leaving her lips. "Why would he have done something like that, John?"

John shook his head. "Who can say? But he didn't have to. He had ample opportunity to sell the cotton. His tip was right, you know. The price of cotton did go up. It climbed on a steady scale until it reached ninety-three cents a pound. I can remember my granddad telling me that Wilson's wife cried and pleaded with him to sell. The family was in dire financial straits. He owed the bank a couple of notes, but he was determined that he would not sell his cotton until the price was a dollar a pound."

"He was really stubborn," Barbara said. "A truly hardheaded man if ever I heard of one."

"He was more than stubborn. He was a little stupid. I mean, the man had a wife and five kids, and he had a chance to make a lot of money, but for several cents he threw it all away. I remember Granddad telling me that story, and I could feel that poor wife's grief. I could hear her begging that man to sell. Granddad was some storyteller. But Wilson didn't sell, and the price started to fall. Ninety cents a pound, then eighty, then fifty, on a downward spiral. And all this time his wife was begging and pleading with him to sell. Then, one night, she had a stroke, and it was all over for her. Wilson was left with the five kids and a hundred bales of cotton that had become almost worthless. I think the day of her burial the price had gone to thirteen cents a pound. Granddad said when Wilson torched that barn with all that cotton inside, the blaze that rose into the sky could have been seen a hundred miles."

Barbara nodded thoughtfully. "Yes. That's where Henrietta stopped yesterday with her part." She laughed gleefully. "She didn't want Miss Hannah to be mad with her for telling too much."

John laughed. "It didn't work, did it?"

"Oh, I think they'll be all right." Suddenly her head tilted. "John, why didn't either of them ever marry?"

"Now that's where the real story is. They both were engaged two or three times each, maybe more. They had callers from all over the state, but the perfect man had to please both of them, plus their father, and that proved to be an impossible task for any man." He reached over to take her hand in his and glanced at her from the corner of his eyes. "Tell me, if a man fell in love with you, how many members of your family would he have to please?"

"One," she answered softly. "Me."

He squeezed her fingers. "That's good news. I would never want to undergo the trials some of my aunts' suitors underwent." Then he lapsed into silence, and they rode the remainder of the way, not speaking, holding hands.

The prison was located in the middle of the delta, stark brick buildings rising out of the flatland, surrounded by fencing on all sides. Upon driving through the gates, Barbara commented, "I wouldn't imagine you have many escapes from here, do you?" There certainly would be no place for an escapee to hide for miles.

"Oh, one or two might try now and then, but it's not a frequent happening."

Barbara waited in a special area while John conducted his business with Lila's husband concerning his parole. Sitting in the waiting room, sipping a Coke, she became extremely thoughtful. She realized she was becoming much too comfortable in the presence of John Michael Stewart, and she sensed he was experiencing the same measure of comfort in her presence.

Suddenly she turned her eyes to the ceiling. He was certainly different from most men she had encountered in the past years. Outside of three kisses he had made no physical advances toward her. And with the one kiss that could have become physical, he had pulled away. How strange. She couldn't help wondering about his reserved nature toward her. She was very relieved and at the same time a little puzzled. If at one time in his life he had lived the playboy lifestyle, it was obviously now a thing of his past.

About an half hour later John came through the door, shaking his head from side to side, his lips drawn into a straight line.

Looking up, Barbara smiled. "How did it go?"

He inhaled deeply. "I suppose we'll know the latter part of this week. His hearing comes up Thursday."

"You look troubled, John," she stated, getting up from the chair and depositing the bottle in the rack beside the machine.

"It took me awhile, but I finally got him to state that he wouldn't write another bad check. The parole board shouldn't hesitate to release him now."

"Oh, good," she said. "Lila will be so thrilled."

Once outside and back in the car, John turned to her. "There's an excellent restaurant on the other side of the river, about forty or fifty miles. Hungry?"

She nodded and smiled, then asked, "Which river?"

"The Ol' Man River," John stated as he turned the key in the ignition.

"Oh, the big one," she said lightly, hoping to elevate his mood.

It was well past dark when they began the trip homeward. Several miles down the highway he reached over and pulled her close to him. She relaxed against his shoulder, smiling contentedly as she stared out at the dark pavement lighted by the headlights of the car. "Was it all you thought it would be?" he asked in a whisper, turning his head and planting a quick kiss on her cheek.

"What?" she said, also in a whisper.

"Prison."

She laughed. "Yes. All I expected and more."

"And the meal?"

"It was very good."

After a slight pause he asked, "And the man?"

With a mock half grimace, she said, "I knew you were asking the easy questions for some reason. So now comes the hard one."

"Is it?"

Still smiling faintly, she glanced at him. "I think you know that I don't have any complaints about the man. In my opinion you are exceptionally good company." She could have easily added, *Intelligent and handsome by any standards*, but she didn't feel it necessary to elaborate.

"Well, let me continue with another one," he said lightly.

"All right, Counselor, go ahead." She chuck-led, softly.

"How do you like the South?"

That one took some thought, for it really caught her off guard. It sounded like the simplest of questions, but she sensed an underlying motive. Finally she said, "From what I've seen, I like it fine."

"We have schools here," he said jokingly. "Did you know that?"

"No," she answered, also jokingly. "I thought education ended at the Mason-Dixon Line."

"We also have schools that teach English courses. That's where I learned to say 'you-all' and 'gosh darn,' and 'yes, ma'am.' Of course, mixed with Shakespeare and Dickens and even Faulkner."

"I'm impressed." She chuckled. "Really I'm impressed."

"Good. That leads me to the granddaddy of all these questions." He cleared his throat dramatically. "Have you ever considered teaching school in the South?"

She laughed loudly. "For goodness' sake, John Michael, no. I have never considered teaching school in the South."

He nodded, his mouth turned upside down. "That's all I wanted to know."

She looked at him, pulling back so that she could get a good view. "Does that mean the questions are over?" she asked, maintaining her lightness.

"For the time being, my dear. I was just more or less trying to get an overview of our situation." With his right arm around her shoulder he hugged her close, then relaxed his hold.

It was past midnight when he turned onto the driveway leading up to the magnificent Stewart house. Pulling to a halt in the front, he killed the motor but made no attempt to open the door. Turning to face her, he spoke in a hushed tone. "I suppose I should thank you for going with me today. You made an ordinary task very enjoyable."

She looked at him but said nothing. The expression on his face was shadowed by the wavering darkness when he spoke. "Barbara, is there anyone special in your life, someone back home?"

"No," she whispered. "There's no one."

He remained motionless, not moving his eyes from her face. "That's good because I would hate to steal someone's dreams from him."

"I don't know that that's possible, John. Is it? To steal someone's dreams?" she said, feeling slightly nervous.

"I suppose what I'm saying, Barbara, is that I'm glad you aren't in love with anyone." He went on as if she hadn't spoken. "Because I think I want you to love me."

Speechless, she stared at him. He thought he

144

wanted her to love him. What a terribly strange thing to say to someone. He definitely had the most unusual approach to love of any man she had ever met or ever heard of. Calmly she moistened her lips and asked, "When do you think you'll know for sure?"

He smiled. "You caught the 'think,' did you?"

"It was hard not to," she answered softly, one side of her mouth curving into a smile.

"Do you care about me, Barbara?" he asked bluntly.

Feeling a hint of panic, she finally whispered uneasily, "Yes."

He cupped her face in warm hands, and she could feel tiny tremors in his fingers.

"I'm happy you do," he murmured close to her mouth. She started to speak, but his kiss hushed her. His lips fiercely smothered her mouth under his, and she faced a moment completely lost from herself. Shocked at the force of his kiss, she did not move, nor did she return his kiss. It seemed that for an eternity she did nothing while his mouth covered hers in a slow, devouring touch, playing slowly, then softly, burning her mouth. Gently her lips parted, and she kissed him back. Her move was followed by a moment of intense pleasure as they fervently rained kisses upon each other's lips. Then he was covering her face, her cheeks, her eyes, down her neck, around to her ear, with a thousand endless hot kisses. Her arms went tightly around

145

his neck as he buried his face against the soft skin of her throat. His touch made her gasp audibly. In that moment he raised his head and looked directly into her eyes, finding her blue irises moist and shiny. With a soft smile he whispered hoarsely, "I only meant to kiss you good night."

"Then maybe that's what you need to do."

He didn't release her. Instead, his embrace slowly tightened. He kissed her again, his lips trembling against hers. Then, suddenly, in one move he released her, reached for the door, and opened it, then slid out and went around to the other side of the car. He stood there for a moment before he leaned down and peered inside at her. Extending his hand, he said in a hoarse whisper, "Let me help you out."

She nodded slowly and whispered, "Thank you."

Minutes later, upstairs in her room, she clutched her head. What in the world was he doing? Did he want to kiss her or didn't he? Oh, she knew he wanted to kiss her; there was no mistaking that fact. Was this some kind of game he played? Shaking her head, she didn't think so. It was something else, something deeper, and she had no inkling what. It was almost as if he were afraid to kiss her. Maybe that was it. Still, nothing about him struck her as being fearful.

After pulling on her gown, she fell across the

bed and lay facedown for a while before slipping over and staring up at the dark ceiling. Everyone in the entire small town knew that he had lived with a woman in this very room. Now she had no doubts that he was attracted to her, so why was he behaving as if he were living in the 1800s instead of the modern world? It was the most frustrating feeling she had known. Not that she was dying to fall into bed with him; that wasn't it, and lucky for her. Then, strangely, as she lay there in the dark, the frustration began to slip away. Maybe that was it. He didn't want an affair with her. Maybe he could look down the road to the weeks ahead when she would be gone and not want to deal with the end of an affair. To her mind that was a plausible explanation.

Closing her eyes, she sighed. The one thing insurmountable to any relationship was absence. And that's what would happen in a few weeks when she left for home. Still, she was a little devastated by her own feelings, a little mixed up. There was something actually happening between her and John. "What if I am falling in love with him?" she said in a whisper. Suddenly her escape South wasn't simple anymore.

The next morning, in her session with Hannah Stewart, her mind kept slipping away from the story being told. More than once she found her-

147

self saying, "Excuse me, Miss Hannah, what did you just say?" She glanced at the older woman and grimaced.

"What's the matter, Barbara, dear?" Hannah peered over the rims of her glasses. "Did John Michael keep you out too late last night?"

Barbara flushed. "No. I don't think that's it."

Hannah smiled and folded her hands together. "You know, Sister and I were talking yesterday about you and our nephew."

Shifting with open discomfort, Barbara bit down on her lower lip.

Hannah went on. "You know, I remember being swept completely off my feet when I met a young man named Homer Waltham for the first time. Even though it was late winter, I recall thinking that it was the first day of real sunshine, the very first day of spring. Do you know why, dear?"

Barbara gave a quick self-conscious shake of her head but made no open answer.

"Because spring comes first to the heart. You can just feel the sun beginning to shine deep inside you, making all nature burst forth. We all are starved for love, but that need is like the empty trees, the bare rose bushes; it has to be awakened by brightness and warmth. And do you know where that brightness, that warmth first appear?"

Again Barbara shook her head one quick time.

"In the eyes," Hannah said with a confident

148

smile. "And that's why Sister and I were talking about the two of you yesterday. She said, 'Hannah, did you see the spark in John Michael's eyes?' And I said, 'I think I did.'" Suddenly she laughed softly. "But that's another story, so why don't we get back to our book? Where were we?"

"You were just telling me about the summer after Mr. Wilson burned the cotton, when all his children became very ill, and then I missed the next thing you said," Barbara admitted, somewhat embarrassed.

Hannah nodded. "Yes." A faraway look filled her eyes. "It was a sad time for the whole town. A terrible flu virus from the Orient swept across this entire country. More than fifty people in this county alone succumbed to it, and three of those were the children of Andrew Wilson. That left him with just his oldest boy, who left home soon after, and poor little Etta, a terribly shy, withdrawn child. I guess she had seen so much tragedy in the past year she couldn't handle it, so she withdrew into her own little world." She gestured with one hand in a loose wave through the air. "And it is at this point that Sister and I can draw from our own observations because we both were in our late teens, added to the fact that it was our own dear father who showed mercy on Andrew Wilson and gave him a few acres to farm and let him live in a small house at the edge of the property."

Barbara glanced up from her notes. "How old was Etta?"

"Fifteen or sixteen, I think."

"Can you describe her, Miss Hannah?"

"Oh, yes. I can see that child as clearly as if it were only yesterday. She had a delicate pale face and long silvery blond hair and large pale blue eyes. Looking at her would somehow remind one of a wisp of the wind, thin and willowy, always wearing a loose-fitting dress that touched her only at the shoulders. A frail child in appearance, but one with a very beautiful face."

Barbara stopped writing and raised her eyes once more. "Miss Hannah, I don't want to get ahead, but tell me, how does this family, this single family, fit into the overall community picture?"

Hannah peered again over the rim of her glasses. "Because, dear, from that sweet child's abdomen came the terror of the county, and it's true even to this day."

Strangely enough, Barbara's thoughts had switched from John Michael to the young woman in the story. She was beginning to get a feeling about the tale she was putting word by word on the note pad, a very strange feeling. Without her knowing why, John Michael's words came tripping across her thoughts: . . . *what goes 'round eventually comes 'round.*

CHAPTER EIGHT

For the next three weeks the trio worked diligently on the story, which was unfolding like one of the full-petaled roses in the vast garden beyond the terrace. John Michael was a regular afternoon visitor to the house after he had closed his office. Often he and Barbara would sit out on the west veranda and drink a glass of Rufus's delicious tea. Rufus's parole had been granted with no problem, and after his release from prison he had taken over most of the cooking and meal preparations, a new skill he had acquired in the prison kitchen. Lila had been freed to take care of the house, and she was continuously cleaning and dusting, humming and singing under her breath.

Barbara looked forward to seeing John Michael. Although she tried to tell herself it didn't matter if he dropped by or not, around four each afternoon she would unconsciously begin glancing at her watch. On this particular afternoon the session with Miss Henrietta had concluded early, and Barbara went out on the veranda to sit in the quiet and gaze at the bright summer day all around her. After many, many hours of her trying to understand John Michael Stewart, she was no closer to her goal than she had been at the beginning of her mental search. He was different; that was the only conclusion she could draw.

This afternoon, when he rounded the corner of the large house, he looked at her and smiled. "Nice day, isn't it?"

She gave a tiny shrug. Regarding him with thoughtful eyes, she saw that he had been home and changed from his usual suit and was spotlessly dressed in creased khakis and a brilliant green pullover shirt. He smiled at her broadly. "How'd the masterpiece go today?"

Her blue eyes sparkled at him. "Excellent. We're well over halfway, I would estimate."

He stood silently, looking at her with an unabashed twinkle in his eyes. "And how disappointed will you be when it's never published?" he asked with a smile.

"Oh, I don't know," she answered rather bluntly. "I think it will be."

He shook his head. "I can assure you that it will not." Pulling up a chair close to her, he sat down.

"John," she said, raising somber eyes to his, "if

you're so certain of that, why are you allowing your aunts to build up their hopes? You know how much this means to them."

He pursed his lips momentarily, then changed the subject completely. "It's such a nice afternoon I thought you might like to go out to the farm and take a horseback ride through the countryside. Want to?"

She looked at him for a few seconds before answering. "Yes, I'd like that," she said, a little startled at the offer. It was the first time he had invited her to his farm. "Let me go upstairs and change into jeans."

During the drive out they discussed the story being told by his aunts.

Her conversation drifted back to the beginning chapters. "Why do you suppose a young woman such as Etta would have a child out of wedlock, John, and never tell anyone one thing about the father? You do realize that it's very much a mystery to people in this area even today?"

"You find it intriguing, don't you?" he asked quietly.

"I've thought about it, John," she answered with some assurance in her tone. "And I've decided that she did it to protect his identity. I don't believe he was a stranger who just happened to be passing through this part of the country. The man who stopped at their house months before the child was born was a scapegoat, and very conveniently so. No one knew who he was or where he came from or even where he went from here. He was seen only that one time, so it's a bit farfetched to me that she would have allowed him to father her child. Your aunts have described her personality to me in detail, and that just doesn't ring true." She shook her head. "No, I think it was someone who spent a great deal of time with her, someone who gained her trust and undoubtedly her love."

"You have given it a bit of thought, haven't you?" He smiled at her.

"When you work with something day in and day out, you begin to get a feeling about it," she replied softly.

"Have you mentioned that possibility to my aunts?" He glanced over at her.

She nodded and smiled. "Yes, but they're certain it was the stranger. In one place they call him the man who brought terror into the county. And after the life the child had I can understand their reasoning. Did he do all the things he's accused of doing?"

John nodded. "As far as I know, Barbara, there's nothing he didn't do. He stole, and he killed two or three men. He actually died in a shoot-out with revenuers over a whiskey still he had already stopped using. Back in those days there was a terrible stigma to being born illegitimate. I suppose they told you of how he slapped the schoolteacher when he was eleven and was never allowed to go back to school?"

"Yes," she said softly. "But the most surprising thing was the fact that he married when he was just sixteen. Somehow I was surprised at that."

"He was human, Barbara. He needed love just like everyone else. You know, by the time he was twenty years old he had four sons—two single births and a set of twins. It was at the birth of the twins that the wife died, and that's when he reverted to his rebellious ways. If she had lived, the entire history of this county might have been different." He shook his head. "But she didn't live, and he reared each of those boys to be filled with more hate than himself, if that's possible. People of this county did live in terror for more than forty years. They never knew what would happen from one day to the next."

"When did it become quiet again?"

He gave a short laugh. "Not that long ago. I guess it was the early sixties when things began to get back to normal. By that time the world had moved in, so when you get down to it, it never really did."

She lapsed into a thoughtful silence just about the time he turned from the highway onto a long asphalt drive which led to a low multilevel brick house situated on a grass-covered hill. "It's very pretty," she said.

"Thank you," he replied softly. "I call it home." He drove past the house and stopped the car a few feet from the barn. A moment later he was around at her side of the car. Reaching out, he took her hand. "Are you wondering why I waited so long to bring you here, Barbara?" he asked with a smile.

She stared at him. "Why did you?"

He chuckled. "Oh, I don't know, maybe I was afraid you would look too good with my house and my barn. You might just add the finishing touch."

Puzzled, she looked into his eyes. "Has anyone ever told you that you're kind of strange, John Michael Stewart?" she asked bluntly.

His eyes shone with delight. "No." He laughed. "You're the first ever to tell me that."

"Well, it's high time someone did."

He bit his tongue sheepishly. "That's because I made a vow to myself a long time ago, a vow I intended to keep."

She looked astounded. "What kind of vow?"

"That the next time I made love to a woman, that woman would be my wife."

Her dark eyebrows soared. "What!"

He nodded with a strained smile. "When my last relationship dissolved, Barbara, I promised myself that it would be my last love affair without marriage."

She peered at him with disbelief. "Why did you do that?" If she had not asked the question, she was sure she would have choked on it.

He peered down at her thoughtfully. "Because I was tired of dealing with broken emotions. I was tired of deceiving and being deceived. I was tired of guilt and self-condemnation. I suppose I was tired of all my trappings. When you reach your thirties, Barbara, the questions take on a different tone. At some point in life you have to face yourself, and that point came in mine. I realized I had made a lot of wrong turns."

"So you chose a life of celibacy?" she questioned, still very much shocked.

Slowly he nodded. "Yes. And with that choice came a peace of mind I'd never known." Suddenly he said excitedly, "I could go on a date, take a woman out to dinner, and expect nothing from her. For the first time in my life I could be friends with the opposite sex without wondering which approach would work best. I could enjoy talking and laughing with no strings attached."

Her gaze swung past him to the barn. "I suppose that's wonderful," she said.

"It's more than wonderful. It's freedom, real freedom. Freedom for myself." He hesitated, then said, "But it doesn't mean I haven't been tempted."

She was now speechless.

"From the moment I walked into my aunts' house and saw you, Barbara, I knew I would undergo my greatest test."

157

"Well"—her voice was back—"I must congratulate you. You've done very well."

"You don't understand, do you?" he murmured very low.

"I'm trying," she answered quickly. "Believe me, I'm trying."

He looked at her for a moment, then said, "I love you." He smiled. "I can say that now because I'm sure I do."

She felt as if the blood had drained out of her head.

His blond hair, mussed by a soft breeze, flew up on one side. He stared at her for a moment, then smiled. "I do," he said softly. "I love you very much."

"John Michael," she said, almost harshly, "how would you know? You've treated me more like a sister than a woman. I'm a woman, with a woman's heart, and a woman's needs, and, yes, a woman's desires! Why didn't you tell me from the onset you had made up your own set of priestly vows?"

"Because I wanted you to be yourself with me. I didn't want to put up a wall between us. I wanted to get to know you, and I have. I know you well enough to know that I love you. And I love you enough to ask you to marry me."

She merely stood staring at him. "Marry you?" she uttered in disbelief.

He nodded boyishly. "I know you need time to think about it, but I wanted to go ahead and ask so that you would have the time." He inhaled deeply. "Barbara, the happiest couple I ever knew was my granddad and grandmother. And you know why?"

She gave one limp shake of her head. "No," she whispered.

"Because they laid the proper foundation for their marriage. Granddad fell in love with her the first time he saw her. He met her in the spring, and for that entire summer he called on her every day. When he would finish with his farmwork, he would go to her house and they would sit outside and drink lemonade or tea, and they would talk. They got to know each other. On weekends he would take her for a buggy ride, and sometimes her brother or sister would tag along, but it didn't matter. He was with her, and that was all that mattered." He stared at her for a moment, then smiled. "And when I'm with you, Barbara, that's all that matters. It's enough merely to know that someday I'll hold you in my arms, that I'll kiss you and not let you go."

"I did not say I would marry you, John Michael Stewart!" She said huffily.

"But you will."

"What makes you so sure of that?"

"Because you love me and because I love you." The next moment he caught her in his arms, staring at her mouth, unmasked desire clearly revealed in his eyes. Then, when she was sure he was about to kiss her, he suddenly dropped his arms from around her and stepped back away from her. Clapping his hands together, he stated, "I'll go saddle the horses."

Astonished, she stared at him for a long moment as he moved in the direction of the barn door. When he disappeared inside, she gave her head several quick shakes. "I'm not marrying you," she muttered under her breath. "There's no way I would marry you. This is not my home." Bracing her hands on her hips, she moaned aloud. Glaring up at a fleecy white cloud floating across the lazy blue sky, she said, "I am not marrying him."

Only a few scant minutes passed before he emerged from the barn, smiling and leading two horses. She stared at him with uncertainty, feeling a bit helpless, a bit wounded, and not at all as sure of herself as she had been only seconds before.

He helped her onto the saddle, then pulled himself up on his own horse. They rode slowly across the rolling hills behind his home, thick, grassy knolls, which for some reason began to emit a certain feeling of tranquillity. Scanning the horizon, she stared over the land, the rich green pastures with cows here and there munching the grass. Looking across at him, she studied his profile for a moment before he glanced and smiled at her. She quickly snatched her head away.

After riding several miles, he pulled on the reins and drew his mount to a halt. "Want to stretch your legs a minute before we ride back?"

"I suppose so," she mumbled. She halted her horse, and slid from the saddle before he could come over to assist her. They walked a little before they reached an isolated oak tree, where he sat down in the grass and looked up at her.

Finally she sat down a few feet from him. He stretched his lean body out in the grass, rolled over onto his stomach, propped himself up, and looked at her. He smiled. "When you get over being upset with me, you're going to realize that I'm offering you more than marriage, Barbara." He pulled up a blade of grass and began to tear it apart. "I'm offering you love, security, friendship. In short, Barbara, I'm offering you all of me."

"I'm confused, John Michael. All this is so sudden. Give me a chance to sort things out."

He continued to tear the blade of grass. "I realize that love is more than a commitment, Barbara. It's more than a word; it's more than an emotion—it's an act of will."

"What do you mean?" she asked, even though she didn't want to talk to him.

"It means I choose to love you. When I first realized my attraction for you, I could have backed off, stayed away, made a choice not to love you, but I didn't. And if I now choose to love you, then I have made my choice for life,

161

for I will love you not only today and tomorrow but always." His words grew softer and lower. "If you would make the same choice, I know we could have a happy future."

"What about my home? What about my work?"

His eyes were suddenly very serious. "That's where your act of will comes in. If you choose to return to your home, to your work, then it'll be obvious that you choose not to love me."

"It's not so cut-and-dried as that," she argued softly.

"There's no big rush. You have a few weeks left before you return home. I want you to have plenty of time to think about it. We both know it's a very big decision, one we'll both live with the remainder of our lives, regardless of your answer."

When they arrived back at the house, he took care of the horses first. When he came out of the barn, he said, "Why don't I throw a couple of steaks on the grill?"

She nodded.

It was dark by the time he served the steaks on the patio table behind his house. They sat quietly at the table, neither one saying much to the other, both enjoying the unhurried meal. The night was especially still, the half-moon shining down on their heads. She gazed at him. "It's so quiet here. You can't even hear the sound of traffic."

He met her look steadily. "I was hoping you would like it."

Something about his expression wrenched her heart. "I do like it," she said tenderly. "I like it very much."

He reached out and took her hand, turned the palm up, and kissed it. "And what about the man?"

She squeezed her lids shut and held them tight for a moment. "I like the man very much."

He gently pressed her fingers, saying, "And if during your search you should discover that you also love him?"

She pulled her hand away from his. She shook her head, her expression one of confusion. Suddenly her throat ached, and for the first time she realized how great was her longing for him, her longing to hold him close, to have him hold her close, to possess, to be possessed.

Without another word he rose from the table, picked up some of the dishes, and began to walk slowly toward the patio door. After lifting the glasses, she followed, reaching out and sliding the door open for him. When he turned from the counter and looked at her, she knew in that instant that his resolutions were about to crumble. She could see the terrible longing in his eyes. And then his face was coming close to hers, and in that moment she didn't care that he was losing his control. Raising her head to meet his,

163

she tasted his lips, softly, tenderly, covering his mouth with no reserve, no care.

He bent his head and returned the kiss with a tenderness matching hers. He pulled back momentarily, and she saw the brilliance of his deep blue eyes. And the caution was lost, swept away by the rush of turbulent emotions. Her hands spread along his chest as bodies drew together. Mouths rained fire, crushing against each other, over and over until gasping, uneven breaths burned them apart. Then their eyes met and held for the longest moment, and they both knew decisions were being made. His fine, soft lips brushed hers again, and she felt the quiver from his body as his arms embraced her, wrapping around her firmly, his hands moving slowly over her blouse, along her ribs and around to the buttons. Lips were soft and welcoming each other as they kissed again and again. Then his hands were inside her blouse, his mouth on her neck, swift, wetting kisses. His hands, with tender strokes, moved up and down, caressing her flesh with a sudden whip of passion.

Her hands slid into his thick hair, touched, pressed his neck, his scalp, and then he murmured against her mouth, "Let's go upstairs, Barbara. . . . Barbara . . ."

The sound of his voice snapped her from the spell binding her to him. Her eyes opened, and she stiffened in his arms. Her thoughts were one big blur.

"Come with me," he murmured, drawing her even closer to him, searching her face through half-lidded eyes.

"No, John." Her words faltered as she gazed at him seriously. "I don't think so. I think you'd better take me home."

A long silence followed. Then his arms dropped away from her. Turning her back to him, she began to rebutton her blouse and after a few moments looked across her shoulder at him. He stood motionless, staring at her. "I—I don't know what to say," he whispered awkwardly.

"I do," she replied very softly. "You almost blew your wedding night." Smiling, she said in a teasing voice, "I don't believe I'm going to want any other woman to be there."

The light reappeared in his eyes. "Are you saying you'll?"

"I'm not saying anything definitely." She smiled. "But I am becoming more open to your proposal as time goes by." Pushing her blouse back inside her jeans, she whispered, "However, you need to take me home."

He nodded, a soft smile curving his lips, a glowing light filling his eyes.

Minutes later, on the highway back to the Stewart house, she smiled at him. "Tell me how India separated you from your millionaire status."

He shook his head slowly and sighed. "You

remember my telling you about Frank Perry?" She nodded, and he went on. "Well, he was into mysticism. That's how he could walk around as if nothing on the face of the earth bothered him. I really admired him, admired the way he appeared to handle everything thrown at him. But tell me, Barbara, why aren't we talking about us? To me that's more important than telling what happened to me in India four years ago."

She gave a slight shake of her head. "I don't want to talk about us right now. I don't even want to think about us. Go on, tell me about Frank."

Somewhat hesitantly he began again after exhaling a long, deep breath. "Well, one day he came to me and said he was going to India. He had made arrangements for instructions under his own personal guru. Everything is personal these days—your personal banker, your personal broker—and he had his own personal guru. To make a long story short, he asked me if I wanted to go along, maybe get my thoughts all straightened out about a lot of things that were bothering me after my dad's death."

"So you went with him?"

He gave one quick up and down of his head. " 'Fraid so. The most costly venture I ever undertook. I was taken in at first, lock, stock, and barrel. I fell for the whole nine yards. But you should have seen the guru. This humble, soft-spoken, bald, bearded old guy, who was willing

166

to share the secrets of the universe with us. Of course, we first had to cleanse ourselves, purge the old life, and that meant getting rid of evil, smelly money."

"What brought you to your senses, John?"

"One day I just decided to go to Calcutta. I'd heard so much about the place I wanted to see it for myself. I tell you, Barbara, it made me ill. Never, never had I seen or imagined such poverty. The stench would kill you. There were little kids running around in filth, living on the streets. Over and over I kept trying to fit this picture in with the one our guru had been trying to put before our eyes. Looking at that terrible poverty, I wondered if my guru really had all the answers after all. And then I saw that the only people there really trying to help were foreigners, Americans, British. It seemed like a nation without hope. And then I started thinking about home. I know everything's not perfect with this country of ours, but compared to what I was looking at, it was almost perfect. Our ghettos are bad, but at least we make some attempt to keep people from starving to death. People here are at least concerned that we have people living in the streets. My granddad used to tell me we lived in a blessed land, but I didn't believe it, not until I walked down those streets of Calcutta. Then I believed it. And in that moment I knew I had been brought up with the truth. I had known the truth all my life but had forgotten it. I started thinking about Aunt Henrietta and Aunt Hannah and my dad's last wish that I look out for them. Believe me, I couldn't get back to the South fast enough." He smiled at her. "You know most of the rest. I opened my office, and here I've been ever since."

"And have you been happy since you came back home, John?"

"I've been content, content enough not to want to leave again." He hesitated. "I don't think anyone is ever truly happy living alone."

"And you weren't bitter about losing your money?"

"At first, but after a while I realized I had a good living, more than I needed to be comfortable. You know dreams and goals are a part of life, a very important part, so when I found myself with mine all shattered, I just picked myself up and selected some new dreams. I'd had the world, and it didn't make me happy. It merely made me a little crazy."

She laughed softly. She studied him for a moment before saying, "You're very sure of yourself now, aren't you? You're sure of what you want in life, even what you need?"

Looking at her, he whispered, "Yes, I'm very sure."

They both were surprised, when they drove up to the house, to see Miss Henrietta and Miss Hannah sitting out on the front porch in cane-bottom rocking chairs, both rocking slowly back and forth. "What time is it?" Barbara asked, surprised almost speechless.

"Ten-thirty." John chuckled.

"They're usually in bed long before now," Barbara commented as he killed the motor. She reached for her door and swung it open.

John alighted from his side of the car and greeted his aunts warmly. "Hello, Aunties. Nice night, isn't it?"

"Young man, get yourself up on this porch this minute."

He glanced quickly at Barbara, trying to maintain a straight expression. "What is it?" he said with wide-eyed innocence.

"We want to talk to you."

"Yes. What is it?"

"It's something Rufus told us after dinner tonight."

Caught off guard, John Michael asked, "What?"

"Well," Henrietta said crisply, "first I want to know if we could sue one of our employees."

"Sue?" His brow wrinkled. "Which employee? Rufus?"

Emphatically, Hannah said, "Yes. He has slandered the Stewart name beyond repair. Sister and I want to know what legal steps we should take before he spreads that terrible lie through the county."

John Michael shrugged. "Well, since he could only write you a bad check, I doubt it would be worth the trouble it would take to start litigation against him. You could fire him, I suppose."

"Oh, no!" Henrietta exclaimed. "We could never do that to poor Lila. She can't help what terrible lies come out of that man's mouth."

Throwing out both hands, he said, "Well, tell me what Rufus said. Then I'll tell you what alternatives you have. All right?"

The two women looked at each other. Finally Henrietta said, "He said our brother . . . our brother . . . Clinton Stewart—oh, I just can't bring myself to repeat it."

"It was just a lie!" Hannah said firmly. "That's what he learned in prison. He was down there with one of those Wilson men who's serving a life term."

Barbara noticed the expression on John Michael's face change radically. All the laughter and joking were gone, and he eyed the two women with dead seriousness. Finally he said, "Rufus told you that Clinton was the father of Etta Wilson's child." Shaking his head from side to side," he added softly. "I didn't want you ever to know, but I'm afraid it's true."

CHAPTER NINE

Pandemonium reigned in the Stewart house for the next few days. Barbara felt completely helpless. Within the first forty-eight hours the Stewart women's responses to the news had been many and varied: disbelief, tears, astonishment, fear, and finally horror. On the third day John Michael came up to her office on the third floor and found her sorting through the papers on the desk. After tapping on the door, he opened it and entered. "What are you doing?" he asked softly. The obvious strain of the ordeal was plain on both their faces.

She quietly answered, "I'm cleaning up. My notes have been destroyed, and Miss Hannah instructed me this morning to tear up the manuscript."

He walked up behind her and put his hands on her shoulders, and she felt the gentle

171

squeeze of his fingers biting softly into her flesh. "I'm sorry," he said with emotion.

Her head tilted upward, a question in her eyes. "Are you?" she asked simply.

He nodded very slowly, looking down to meet her eyes. "I'll admit, Barbara, I didn't want the book to be written, but when I saw that they were going ahead with it, I backed off and reconsidered. I could see it was beneficial to both of them to be caught up in a new interest. However, had they completed it, I would have fought against its publication."

"Why, John?" she asked.

He paused and considered his words. "Because of the harm they would suffer. You see, Barbara, the fact that Clinton Stewart fathered that child is not the secret my aunts believed it to be. It's not public knowledge, but a fair number of people know it. The truth is, they have been protected from the truth, first by their father and over the years by others."

"It's incredible that it could have been kept from them all these years."

"Not when you consider their lives. They have been very private people. Most of their activity has been at the church." Releasing her shoulders, he walked over, took a straight chair by the back, and positioned it next to hers. After he had sat down, he rubbed his face with both hands. "Were you surprised, Barbara?"

"Yes and no," she said. "I was surprised to

discover it was a Stewart, but I had never believed it had been that stranger. After learning of Etta Wilson, I knew instinctively that no stranger could have earned her confidence in the span of a few hours." The concern in her eyes deepened. "Why didn't he marry her, John?"

He shook his head slowly, and his eyes narrowed thoughtfully. "I don't know. Maybe he was frightened, maybe ashamed, maybe both. And maybe it was some other reason or a combination of other reasons. It happened so many years ago the truth has been lost. But I do know that at some point money passed from the Stewarts to the Wilsons."

"How do you know?"

"My granddaddy told me. You see, he was Clinton's brother. He told me that their daddy gave Andrew Wilson enough money to leave the county, but old Andrew pulled a fast one on him. He took the money and bought back his hundred acres of land, and the Wilsons still have it to this day."

"Somehow it seems unfair," Barbara whispered. "Unfair to that girl, unfair to her child, unfair to all the generations since then."

He leaned forward toward her. "Yes, it was unfair, but it happened."

"And it's over and done with," she added as an afterthought.

"It'll never be over with. It'll go on and on as

long as there is a Stewart or a Wilson left in this county."

She smiled. "I think I'll give up my ghost-writing career."

"I hope." He laughed.

She raised her brows thoughtfully. "What is going to happen to poor Rufus? Neither of your aunts has spoken to him in three days now."

He gritted his teeth playfully. "They're talking to him now. He went out this morning and bought both of them new recliners for their parlor. I just left them all downstairs, and believe me, he's forgiven."

Barbara laughed softly. "I'm happy. It's been miserable at meals. The way they looked at him, you would have thought he was the one responsible." Suddenly she pulled back and gazed at him strangely. "How did he pay for the recliners?"

"How do you think?" John asked calmly.

"Not with a check!" Barbara exclaimed.

John Michael said matter-of-factly, "Not just with a check, Barbara, but with a bad check, six hundred dollars' worth to be exact. That's why I'm here. I came to send the chairs back."

"Oh." She sighed, unable to keep the smile from her lips.

He inhaled deeply. "When I saw that the chairs had bridged the troubled waters, I told Rufus I would make this one check good for him. But I also told him if he ever did it again, I would

174

personally drive him back to prison myself and deposit him there and forget about him. I think he believed me this time."

"I hope so." Barbara laughingly leaned over and buried her face against his shoulder. "You have a hard time with your clients, don't you?"

His fingers stroked her short dark hair. "When you're in love, you hardly notice the minor things."

"So I've found out," she whispered.

That night they sat at dinner with his two aunts, each of whom was beginning to deal with the shock of nights before. Rufus came in, carrying a platter of fried chicken, and smiled sheepishly at one lady, then the other. Then he looked at Barbara and John, who were seated at the opposite side of the table. "You two sure are dressed fit to kill tonight," he commented dryly, obviously still miffed at his attorney.

Barbara wore a slim-fitting dress of deep blue, and John Michael sat attired in a black suit and white open-necked dress shirt. He looked lean and handsome. Both women scrutinized them after Rufus had returned to the kitchen and then turned and smiled knowingly at each other.

After the meal, while still at the table, John Michael lifted his napkin and slowly wiped his mouth. With a soft smile on his face he said, "If you don't mind, I think I'll prepare us an after-dinner drink." Before anyone could agree, he was up from his chair and out of the room. In a minute or two he was back carrying a tray of glasses. His blue eyes gleaming brightly, he placed the drinks from the tray on the table. Then, smiling broadly, he returned to his seat. Clearing his throat and squaring his shoulders, he said, "Aunt Henri, Aunt Hannah, I would like you to be the first to know that Barbara and I are going to be married." He met both their gazes with his own penetrating look and smiled in response to their smiles. It was obvious to Barbara that they both were a little amazed by the announcement, and for a moment she could not tell what they were thinking or feeling.

John Michael laughed, saying, "Aren't you going to say anything?"

Henrietta spoke first in a very low voice. "I'm so happy for you, both of you."

Hannah nodded, then glanced uneasily at her sister before looking back to Barbara. "I hope you never regret your decision, dear, for young people should be married. John Michael has brought so much happiness to our lives."

"Yes," Henrietta added softly. "I still remember the day Sister and I realized that our youth was gone, and our hearts were numb, and our arms were empty. All our chances at happiness had passed us by. And then John Michael came home and filled some of the emptiness we had known for years. Now, it's only fair to both of you that we let him go."

"Hey," John Michael said firmly, "what is this? Are you two trying to get rid of me?"

Near tears Hannah said, "We knew this day would come someday, and we're very happy for you, John Michael." Then she turned to Barbara. "And you, too, Barbara, dear." She hesitated, then went on in a fearfully low voice. "I suppose this means you'll be returning to New Jersey."

Barbara nodded, her eyes beginning to moisten. "Yes. I want to be married at home in my church."

"We understand," Henrietta said pitifully, then paused and looked at her sister.

John Michael suddenly clapped his hands together. "And that brings up the next question: How would you like to travel to New Jersey for our wedding?"

Both faces underwent an instant uplift. "New Jersey? Us?" Henrietta exclaimed.

He nodded. "You don't want me up there all by myself, do you? I mean, Barbara will be there with all her family. I want my family there too." Suddenly his eyes glistened under the light from the chandelier. "You won't be losing a nephew, you know; you'll be gaining a niece. We'll both be here, right here, as long as either of you need us."

Barbara wiped at her eyes as inconspicuously as possible. "Yes." She whispered her agreement. "After all, you're responsible for our meeting."

Henrietta looked at her sister. "And to think, Hannah, only this afternoon we were talking about what a terrible idea the book had been."

John Michael smiled. "It was the best idea you ever had, for all of us."

Hannah picked up her glass of wine and looked first at her sister, then at the pair across from her. "I would like to propose a toast," she said, her voice shaky with emotion. "From Sister and me, we both wish you all the happiness two hearts can hold."

"And all the love two arms can enfold," Henrietta said tearfully.

After the toast had been drunk, Hannah turned to her sister, saying, "Did you notice that our toast made a rhyme, Sister?"

Henrietta mouthed the words over again silently. Then her expression perked up. "Why, we surely did, and quite accidentally I might add."

"Maybe your writing careers aren't ended after all." John Michael chuckled happily. "Maybe you were meant to be not novelists but, rather, poets."

Their expressions growing brighter with each passing moment Henrietta said, "That would be wonderful, wouldn't it? We know so much about life. Yes, I think maybe we will consider poetry."

Hannah's eyes filled with tears once again. "I

178

would like our first poem to be for our dear brother Clinton. He was so unhappy in his short life, and Sister and I never knew the source of his sorrow. Now that we know, I believe we could write something very fitting for our brother."

Dabbing at her eyes, Henrietta agreed. "Yes. That's where we'll begin. We'll begin with Clinton."

Following the get-together with his aunts, John Michael asked Barbara if she would like to walk outside. The night was especially peaceful and still, the moon shining full overhead, millions of stars shining brightly against a velvety black backdrop. Holding hands, they walked quietly along the path beyond the west rose garden, past the gap in the hedge to the towering oak where Barbara had sat reading. Finding a grassy spot, John Michael took off his coat and spread it over the ground, and they both sat down close to each other yet not touching. She smiled at him and said softly, "It went well with Miss Henri and Miss Hannah, didn't it?"

Smiling, he gazed at her face. "Yes. But I never doubted it for a moment. I could tell from the onset that they were very fond of you."

She pinched his arm lovingly. "There you go with that word again."

He met her look teasingly. "What, 'fond'? I'm still fond of you myself."

She returned his gaze steadily. "If you've

gone through life using that word with your women friends, little wonder you're still single at thirty-four."

He grinned. "What makes you think I've ever used it before?"

Her eyes shone brilliantly in the natural light from the heavens. "Oh, I have the feeling that must have been one of your approaches. You did say you had different approaches with different women." She laughed softly. "That must have been your southern gentleman act. My dear," she drawled with an exaggerated flair in her tone, "I, John Michael Stewart, am terribly . . . terribly . . . f-o-n-d of your sweet self."

His brows rose sharply. "Hey, for a little Yankee girl that's not bad." White teeth sparkled in the darkness. "As a matter of fact, with a little practice you might just master it. Here, let me help you." Taking her face with both hands, he rounded his mouth in an oblong *O* shape. "Start like this. Then bring our lips slightly closer, and go, 'Faa . . . fa . . . faond.'"

She began laughing. "Let go of my face, you lunatic."

"Ah, now you're getting closer. But did you know that we lunatics are extremely influenced by a full moon?"

"Well, don't get any ideas," she whispered in a seductive tone, "because full moon or not, you started this thing, but if necessary, I'll finish it. You said you would not make love again until you made love to your wife." She tilted her head slightly and pursed her lips in a mock kiss.

He was perfectly still, watching her. "I love you, Barbara."

"And I love you, John. I love you so very much, and I love your aunts, and I love Lila, and I even love poor Rufus. I feel so full of love my heart could almost burst from it." Tenderness filled her eyes.

Leaning forward, he kissed her cheek, then the tip of her nose. "Tell me, are you the prettiest Whitney girl?"

"We all resemble each other, as you'll soon find out."

"But you're the prettiest, aren't you?"

"John"—she sighed with some frustration—"how do you expect me to answer that?"

He grinned. "Well, you could be kind and say no, or you could be vain and tell the truth. But I already know you are."

She raised her brows. "And what if you find out that I'm not?"

His grin broadened. "Then I'll take you anyway." Bending forward, he kissed her neck, and she felt a chill sweep down her back. Her eyes closed, and her arms went around his neck. She put her head on his shoulder, quite content to remain that way forever. It was such a perfect, peaceful moment. They held each other, relaxed and content for a long, long time.

That night, after he had gone home and she

was upstairs, she put on her gown and sat down on the side of her bed. Her fingers strayed into the sides of her hair, and she smiled to herself, thinking, thinking of the time past, thinking of the time ahead. Life was strange indeed. She had come to this small southern town to seek solutions to the problems plaguing her life, and strangely enough, she hadn't found the solution at all but had found life itself. She had come to realize that love was life; without it there was only existence.

CHAPTER TEN

It was a traditional wedding with traditional vows that took place in a neighborhood church in one of the suburbs of Trenton, New Jersey. It was late Saturday afternoon near the end of August when the relatives and friends of Barbara Whitney and John Michael Stewart gathered to witness the ceremony which took two unrelated people and made them one person, which took people from different parts of the country and magically sealed them into one family.

Barbara was nearly numb from the excitement. Since their arrival in New Jersey a week earlier she had run and visited and been the recipient of bridal showers, and it was only in those quiet moments in the dressing room of the church with her mother and oldest sister assisting her with her bridal gown that the full impact of the event struck her. Her hands began to tremble slightly; then the tremble diffused throughout her body.

Fastening the many tiny pearl buttons at the back of the lace bodice, her mother asked softly, "Barbara, are you nervous?"

"A little," Barbara whispered, trying to swallow around the sudden dryness of her throat.

Turning to Barbara's sister, Mrs. Whitney said, "Brenda, finish with these buttons, and let me go find Barbara some water, and I want to check to see if your father is where he needs to be."

"Sure," Brenda replied, and walked over to work on the buttons about midway down Barbara's back. "It's a very pretty dress," she commented while busily at work.

"Thank you," Barbara replied. "You know his aunts made it. I told you, didn't I?"

"Where in heaven's name did they get the pattern? I haven't seen a dress like this from anywhere."

"From a trunk in the attic. It was either Miss Henri's or Miss Hannah's. I don't think they knew for sure." She smiled. "There were several patterns in the trunk."

When she finished with the last button, Brenda stepped back and said, "Now turn around, and let me look at you."

Slowly Barbara turned, her eyes wide in anticipation.

Brenda smiled. "It's beautiful. You, too, little sister." She began straightening the long skirt of satin and lace, smoothing out the folds. Glancing up at Barbara, she asked, "Are you looking forward to your honeymoon?"

Smiling, Barbara answered, "Yes." Then she elaborated. "For the first week or so we'll be at home; then we're taking a Caribbean cruise."

"I still don't understand why you're not taking the cruise first?"

"We want to do it this way," Barbara smiled softly. "First we're going home."

It was past 2:00 A.M. when John Michael pulled the rental car into the drive of the Stewart home to let off his aunts. Barbara stayed in the car while he assisted them with their luggage. Both women followed him back to the car and peered inside, Henrietta saying to Barbara, "Dear, Sister and I would be happy to fix you something to eat or make you some tea if you'd like."

Seeing John Michael's look of consternation, Barbara chuckled softly. "It's so late, I suppose we should be getting on home," she answered.

Hannah yanked at Henrietta's sleeve and whispered, "Sister, I'm surprised at you. Do you think they want to spend their wedding night in our dining room?"

"Oh." Henrietta's hand flew to her mouth. Then she stepped back from the door of the car and said, "Good night, children."

John Michael slid back inside the car and

closed the door. Watching the house until both his aunts were inside, he turned to Barbara. "Have you ever seen an attorney panic?" he asked matter-of-factly but with a sly grin on his lips.

Barbara burst out laughing. "And if I had been hungry or thirsty and accepted their sweet invitation, you would have panicked?"

"No." He gave a quick shake of his head. "I would have fallen down onto their dining room floor and died."

Reaching over and squeezing his arm, she laughed gleefully. "You aren't saying you're anxious to get home, are you, Mr. Stewart?"

"No, not I," he said with great exaggeration. "I mean, we've only been through our wedding ceremony, the reception, the four-hour flight, the thirty-minute drive. I'm in great shape for a man who just had a close call, a man who almost spent the remainder of his wedding night in his aunts' dining room."

Laying her head on his shoulder, she realized how utterly free she felt, how uninhibited, how wonderfully secure.

Taking her time in the bathroom adjoining the bedroom, Barbara began to feel the first pangs of apprehension. Really they began when she closed the bathroom door. The warm shower helped, and after drying off, she reached for her gown and negligee. Again her hands be-

186

gan to shake a little, as was obvious when she lifted a small bottle of perfume from her case. Finally she knew she could delay the moment no longer, and slowly her hand reached for the door. In the first step she caught sight of him sitting patiently on the side of the bed, waiting for her. From the moment she looked at him she could see nothing else; nothing else existed.

Dressed only in the bottoms of pale blue pajamas, he sat straight-shouldered with his hands folded neatly in his lap. His hair, wet from the shower, was neatly groomed with a razor-sharp part. His bright blue eyes caught hers and held them firmly. She noticed the unusual flush in his cheek, the tight expression on his face. He was nervous. She felt it first in the depths of her being, and then she felt the corners of her mouth begin to curl upward with a smile of love for him.

She heard his faint murmur. "You're beautiful." Then she glimpsed the bottle of champagne and the two glasses on a small silver tray on the bedside table.

"You've been busy, haven't you?"

When she sat down beside him on the bed, he handed her a glass half filled and lifted the other for himself. She sat staring at him with her mouth slightly open, tenderness in her eyes. He cleared his throat, and his words emerged in a hoarse whisper. "I thought we might want to begin this night with a toast."

"Yes." She agreed lovingly, quietly her eyes sweeping over his face.

His head turned toward her, and he drew in a long breath, smiling wryly. "I think the nicest words coming to my mind are really very simple ones, yet they say so much." He spoke so gently and tenderly that her heart began to knock frantically against her chest wall. "To . . . my wife."

"The most beautiful words in the world," she said, lids lowered, a happy flush on her cheeks.

He turned abruptly and lowered his face to hers, catching the curve of her lips softly with his mouth at the same moment his hands reached for her glass. While he kissed her, he blindly returned the glasses to the tray. With that first touch she felt locked to him forever. Her hand came up to touch his hair, quivering fingers sinking into the soft strands. So many beautiful, wonderful sensations filled her, flowing through her, washing over her.

He wrapped his arms about her, and his lips were at her throat, sweeping the delicate hollow at its base, her neck, lingering on the smooth skin of her shoulder. The touch of his hands, the feel of his mouth, the warmth, the love. His fingers went inside the negligee to the satiny straps of her gown, sliding, managing to free her smoothly. Burying his face between her neck and shoulder, he caressed her bare back, then came around to the sudden hardness of her

breasts. The night around them disappeared behind the blindingly bright flash of desire. It was
new. Yes, to her it was new, a feeling, a sensation
she had not dreamed existed, a staggeringly
powerful emotion which just reached out and
enveloped her, pressing her desire to his and his
to hers, as if between the two of them a new
power had been born, of passion, of desire, of
oneness.

She had no idea when they were no longer
embracing, no idea how her head came to be on
the soft pillow. She just knew that he was there,
his face hovering so close to hers, looking into
her eyes, his own eyes burning with a brilliance,
filling with ecstasy. Her arms went up around
his neck and brought his mouth down to hers.
All her wishes and dreams of life were being
fulfilled. This wasn't a moment of passing weak-
ness, a moment of mind becoming ruled by
body. This was a commitment, an act of two
wills, and it was real. All past illusions were
swept away by the reality of a true love, one
which would last a lifetime. As long as they
lived, they would have this unblemished night
between them. This was their creation. They
had chosen it.

Her arms and legs were around him, tying
him to her, reeling together on the buoyant
waves of love. She would never again not know
him: the leanness of his body; the burning moist-
ness of his lips; the firmness of his abdomen; the

hardness which shaped and molded him into the man he was. This was becoming one. They could never be closer—or more. They were complete.

"I love you so much, Barbara," John murmured against her lips.

Still floating in a whirling splendor, she returned the words. "And I love you, John."

He lay back beside her, one arm under her neck and draped over her shoulder, smiling at her contentedly. She was hardly conscious of anything but his nearness. Closing her eyes, she knew she had been granted the best of everything life had to offer, and on this foundation they would build the remainder of their lives—together.

"What are you thinking?" he whispered hoarsely.

Peering at him from the corners of her eyes, she grinned and said, "I was thinking how fa . . . fa . . . faond I am of you."

Laughing with delight, he raised himself up on one elbow and peered back at her. "You got it! That was it!" Bending down to kiss the tip of her nose, he said, "Just think, during this week I can teach you to say 'you-all,' and—"

Laughingly she silenced him by placing her lips against his in a quick kiss, then said, "I know . . . and 'gosh darn' . . ." The rest of her words died beneath his kiss.

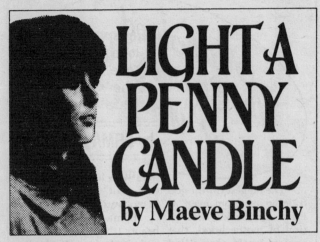

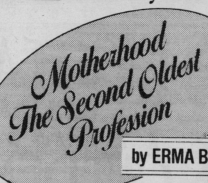